PRAISE FOR THE
APPALACHIAN MOUNTAIN MYSTERIES

"GREAT !! BOOK Lynda McDaniel can write. This is one fine read. Reads like a literary piece." —**Wooley, Amazon Vine Voice Reviewer**

"I COULD NOT PUT THIS BOOK DOWN!" —**J. Capella, Amazon bestselling author of *Your Dream Team***

"FIVE STARS! Lynda McDaniel has that wonderfully appealing way of weaving a story, much in the manner of Fannie Flagg. The tale immediately drew me in, into the town, into the intriguing mystery, and into the people. A real treat to read and made me anticipate meeting the characters in yet another installment." —**Deb, Amazon Hall of Fame Top 100 Reviewer**

"THE MOST SATISFYING MYSTERY I'VE READ IN AGES." —**Joan Nienhuis, 1% Top Reviewer Goodreads**

"GREAT PACING—I couldn't put it down. I highly recommend this book, but read *A Life for a Life* first, so you can truly appreciate all that Abit accomplishes in *The Roads to Damascus*." —**Malena E., author and playwright**

Your free book is "Waiting for You."

Want to spend more time with Abit Bradshaw and Della Kincaid? Get your free copy of the prequel novelette, *Waiting for You*.

I've pulled back the curtain on their lives before they met in Laurel Falls—between 1981 and 1984. You'll discover how Abit lost hope of ever having a meaningful life and why Della had to leave Washington, D.C.

Haven't started the series yet? ***Waiting for You*** will get you started in style.

Get your free copy of *Waiting for You* here:
https://www.lyndamcdanielbooks.com/free

The Roads to Damascus

A Mystery Novel

Lynda McDaniel

This novel is a work of fiction. Any references to real people, events, establishments, organizations, or locales are intended only to give the fiction a sense of reality and are used fictitiously. All others are products of the author's imagination.

Published in 2018 by Lynda McDaniel Books.

The Roads to Damascus Copyright © 2018 by Lynda McDaniel

ISBN: 978-0-9977808-4-0

Printed in the United States of America

*Dedicated to everyone
who's taken the hero's journey.*

*"It is God's kindness to terrify you
in order to lead you to safety."* – Rumi

October 1989

Chapter 1

"Della, open up. I'm in a mess of trouble."

Jake was whining at the screen door, as happy to see me as I was him. While I was whispering what a good boy he was, I could hear Della in her office talking on the phone, so I figured she didn't hear us carrying on.

I couldn't talk too loud since I didn't want Mama or Daddy to know I was back in Laurel Falls. At first when I went off to school about four year ago, I'd come home most weekends. (The school was a ways up the road in Boone, N.C.) But as I got to liking what the school offered, I rarely came home more than oncet a month.

I'd've visited more if I could've just hung out with Della Kincaid (who owned the store next door to my family's house), but I had to stay with Mama and Daddy. Mama fussed over me and worried about what I was getting up to in the "big city," and Daddy still ignored me. Not so much out of disgust, more like habit.

"Della!" I said as loud as I felt was safe. "It's me, Abit."

She came into the living room all smiles, her arms wide open, ready for a big hug after she unlocked the screen door. "Hey, honey," she said, throwing her arms round me. "I was on the phone with Alex. He had to go back to D.C. to meet with one of his editors. What brings you here at this hour?"

"I guess you didn't hear me. I got thrown out of school, and I need your help."

Chapter 2

My troubles started about four months earlier when a girl came skipping over the mountainside where I was tending the cows. She'd put some violets in her long blond hair, and they matched the flowers on her gauzy dress. Truth be told, I thought I was seeing something from the spirit world. I blinked a time or two, not believing my eyes, but she was still there.

I was at the Hickson School of American Studies in a work/study program, something they offered folks like me who had a "learning disability"—a couple of words they drilled into us instead of *stupid* or *retard*. The school was part of the university in Boone and named after someone who'd given it a bunch of money. Too bad about his name. The way things like that went, the school's long name kept getting shortened until it was known as simply The Hicks.

For one of my jobs, I tended the cows that were in season at the school dairy. They liked to graze on a grassy slope that faced west toward Beech Mountain, and every Tuesday and Thursday afternoons I kept check on them. I wasn't sure what was the prettiest—the view of the mountains or them Jersey cows with their dreamy brown eyes and long lashes. Mama had a cow for a while, but it was a Holstein, and while they're a fine-looking breed, they aren't gorgeous like these girls. I'd sit among them, not shepherding or anything like that, just keeping an eye out to make sure they were safe. I'd found a good place to sit, where the rocks formed a natural backrest, and I'd lose myself in the gentle lowing from the herd.

So that day, a particularly warm spring day, I was in a kind of daze when that girl appeared. She settled down next to me like an apple blossom fluttering to the ground.

"Hello! I'm Clarice. Who are you?"

"Uh, hi." I felt all tongue-tied, but pretty girls did that to me. I hadn't really had a girlfriend yet—no one back home would give me the time of day, and at The Hicks, there weren't that many girls. Besides, I couldn't imagine anyone would say yes if I asked her out, and I just wasn't up for more rejection.

"I said, who are you?"

I nearabout said Abit, but caught myself. "V.J."

I got that nickname Abit because Daddy told everyone, "He's a bit slow." That made him feel better, letting the world know that he knew he had a retard (his word). Turns out I'm not the sharpest saw in the tool chest, but not the dullest, neither. My teachers have showed me lots of things and helped me appreciate other qualities I have. I just needed someone—make that several someones—to believe in me.

Thing was, that school was everything I'd hoped it would be. I hadn't done so well in public school back in Laurel Falls, so again, to make himself feel better, Daddy took me out of school when I was twelve. But after that summer of 1985, Alex Covington (Della's ex-husband and later her boyfriend) and Della's best friend Cleva Hall pulled some strings and got me in The Hicks. Alex had even written a book about the place—more like one of them coffee table books with lots of pictures and some stories. (Thank heavens it ended up *not* featuring me, the way he'd threatened.)

"V.J. what?" she asked, snuggling kinda close-like.

"Do you mean what does V.J. stand for or what's my last name?"

"The latter."

That was a relief because I didn't have to tell her V.J. stood for Vester Junior. I hated Daddy's name, and I didn't even want to say it out loud. "Bradshaw. V.J. Bradshaw. What's yours?"

She frowned at me. "Clarice, as I said earlier." I guessed she was just so, well, different lookin', I'd been studying her rather than paying attention to what she'd said. "Ledbetter. Clarice Ledbetter," she added.

We started in talking and oncet we got warmed up, we carried on like old friends. I couldn't believe how much we had in common. When I told her I liked her blond hair, she said she liked my red hair. When she shared how much she loved dogs, I raved about them, too. But when I asked if she'd come for the Dance Week starting the next day—I could already see her dancing in that beautiful dress—her pretty face changed in a flash.

No, she said, her chin quivering, she was here because her mother was dying and the school had been nice enough to rent them the Gate House for the duration. Seemed her mama grew up round the school and wanted to die nearby. Clarice told me all about what medical things were happening to her mama (in more detail, to be honest, than I cared to hear). It was one of the saddest stories I'd heard in some time. No longer killing time out front of Della's store meant I didn't hear all the tales of woe from my fellow bench-sitters.

I wrestled with the fact that Clarice was living with so much sorrow, while I was feeling so happy that such a pretty girl was paying attention to me (even though I figured she just needed someone to talk to). And I liked the idea that she wouldn't be leaving after Dance Week (not unless her mama took a quick turn for the worse). Too often people I enjoyed left after only a week or two; they came for just a short time to learn some of the art and music of the mountains. Way back, the school had started as a settlement school to teach mountain people the ways of the world. Then about thirty year ago, it turned into a place for city folks to come learn *our* ways.

Before long, the sun had slipped behind a mountain. Sunset came early there, the mountains stealing a good couple of hours from our days. Even the swallows were fooled, swooping and soaring as though it were time for their bedtime snack. As much as I wanted to stay (and not because of that sunset), I had to get down to the school kitchen to help the cooks, Lurline and Eva. "Do you take any of your meals with us at the school?" I asked. "I also work in the kitchen, and I could get you some extra helpings." I felt silly as soon as those words were out of my mouth. Even I knew I was groveling. But she smiled and seemed to take it in the right way.

"Thanks, but we can't afford the school's meal plan. I do most of our cooking now."

"Gosh, I'm sorry. I bet I could wrap up some leftovers for you, from time to time. We usually have a lot extra. Lurline and Eva always cook too much, just in case more people show than they expected. And it's a shame for it to just go to the pigs."

"That's real sweet of you, but I wouldn't want to deprive the pigs!" I was about to explain myself when she smiled and kissed me on the cheek. Just then one of them Jerseys let out a big fart, and we both started laughing. I don't know when I've appreciated a fart more, because otherwise, I'd have been sitting there like a fool, dumbstruck by her kiss.

We both stood up, and she brushed some leaves and stuff off her skirt—and my behind! She sure looked good standing there, the breeze catching her hair and rippling that gauzy skirt. "I knew what you meant, V.J., but you don't have to do us any favors. I wouldn't want to get you in trouble."

"Oh, you couldn't get me in trouble," I said. "Besides, I'm sure everyone wants to help you out. We take care of our own."

"But we're outsiders."

"Yeah, but you said your mama was from the area. So that's good enough for me." She smiled again, and I paused for a moment before adding, "I gotta get going. You comin'?"

"No, that dark old cottage depresses me. I believe I'll sit here a while longer and drink all this in," she said, sweeping her hand in the most graceful way.

I loped off, wishing I didn't have to leave. But it would be too obvious to suddenly say *Oh, I don't need to go, after all.*

I met a fair number of people who struck me that way—folks I'd like to know better—but most times they didn't want to know me. Like when I'd call someone and leave a message, but they'd never call back. Sometimes I'd check to see if there'd been an electrical storm that'd turned off my answering machine. Or I'd think maybe the tape had run out. Most times, it hadn't even started.

Other times, I'd see all these folks with big groups of friends, laughing and carrying on, piling into a car to go to the movies or a music gig. They'd wave at me, and I'd wave back, acting like I was real happy for them, heading off to have fun. And I guess I was. I just couldn't figure out why I was only good enough to wave at.

I always saw friendship—like me and Della had—as about the finest thing in the world, and I wanted as much of that as I could get. *Maybe I was trying too hard*, I'd tell myself when things didn't work out. Or, *maybe I said something wrong.*

No wonder, then, I was tickled that Clarice had taken a liking to me. After that first time, I saw her a bunch more at school. We hung out sometimes and had meals together, especially when her brother, Clayne, weren't round. They took turns taking care of their mama back at the cottage and, like Clarice had told me, cooked their own meals, most times. Later on, Clarice worked out some kind of deal doing odd jobs for the school in trade for some meals. "I just *have* to get out of that cottage, sometimes," she whispered oncet when we was sitting next to each other at dinner.

Even though Alex had warned me that Lurline and Eva weren't as good cooks as Mama, I loved those meals. Chicken and dumplings. Macaroni and cheese. Pork chops that weren't cooked to shoe leather. And with Clarice sitting with me, I felt like somebody. Out of all them guys, she chose me. Not that the competition was that stiff. Some of the guys were kinda scruffy and some were too shy to even look at her. But for a while, I felt like the luckiest guy at the school.

Chapter 3

"Well, Mister, I hate to break up this lovefest, but it's getting late," Della said, carrying in a tray of cold chicken sandwiches, potato salad, and coconut cake. She set it on the coffee table.

Jake and I had been tussling on the floor on an oval braided rug she'd added since I was there last. Whenever I came home from The Hicks for a weekend, I tried to spend plenty of time with Jake. I'd trained him to dance on his hind legs and speak for treats, and we'd go for long walks into the woods. Whenever I'd see him after a spell of being away, I noticed how my heart felt fuller when we were together. It felt good, and I found myself wondering what happened to all them feelings when I wasn't with Jake. Were they in there, kinda dormant, like them noisy cicadas that wait seventeen years before they come back? Did the feelings build up between visits and come roaring out when we were reunited? I didn't know the answer, but I wanted them to come out more, even when Jake weren't round.

I sat up, tucked my legs under the coffee table, and started chowing down. I could've eaten every one of them sandwiches, I was so hungry. Della kinda nibbled on one, but she'd probably had her dinner earlier. She let me eat for a while before asking more about what'd happened at the school. I thought for a minute about how to answer her. There were things I wanted to share, and some I just couldn't tell her. Not yet, anyways.

"It started when some people came to the school—a mother, son, and daughter," I said with my mouth full, but Della didn't seem to mind. "The mother was dying, and the two kids were looking after her. They'd moved to the school because they were evicted from somewhere in Virginia 'cause she was too sick to work, and what her son earned wasn't enough to live on." I stopped to eat for a minute, and then added, "She'd growed up nearby our school and wanted to die as close to her family's home place as she could. I remember how tore up we all were listening to her story. A bunch of us had gathered on the front porch of Gate House, where she sat, talking and taking in that heavenly mountain view. It was like she was looking into her future."

While she listened to my story, Della didn't look all that sad. "Let me guess," she said after a while. "They got you to part with some of your hard-earned savings."

"Aw, come on, Della. It wasn't that obvious. You had to be there."

"Okay, you're right. It just pisses me off that they took advantage of you."

"It wasn't just me," I said through another mouthful— this time her homemade coconut cake. "A bunch of us were taken in. But that wasn't the half of it. Most people at the school don't even know what else happened. At least not about them stealing so much money. We all lost some, but old man Henson, the director of the school, lost a lot, and the money wasn't just his. It was the school's, too. At least that's the story goin' round. When someone said we should call the cops, he piped up that it wasn't worth it—crooks like them are next to impossible to catch. Besides, he said he didn't want to shame the school. I think he just didn't want people to know how stupid he'd been with the school's money."

"So, why are *you* in trouble, Abit?"

"Because before they left, they put $2,000 *into* my savings account! I know that sounds even weirder, but it's a long story." I don't know if it was because of the food or the time of night or the fact that I was unloading this burden on my best friend, but I suddenly felt so tired I could hardly finish my cake. I yawned real big, and Della noticed.

"You can tell me more tomorrow. For now, hop into bed in the guest room. It's all made up for you." She hugged me and said goodnight. She closed her bedroom door but then came right back out. "You'll need to clear out by noon tomorrow. I don't want to be sneaking behind Mildred and Vester's backs. You can go home and make it look as though you just walked from the bus station."

"What will I tell them?"

"We'll figure that out in the morning."

Della woke me up with breakfast in bed. I had no idea what that was like, though I'd seen it on TV. (And I sure was glad she'd left off the rose in a vase.) At first I felt like a fool with a tray in my lap, but I had to admit, I got accustomed real fast. She helped me get the pillows right behind my back and arranged the tray just so before pulling up a chair nearby. "I called Alex, and he wants to see you."

20

"OK, when's he coming back? I've got all the time in the world."

"He can't get away. He wants you to come to D.C."

I couldn't speak, and not because I'd just taken a big bite of one of Mrs. Parker's cinnamon rolls. I gulped it down, took a swallow of coffee, but I still couldn't get a word out. I'd never been out of North Carolina, let alone to the nation's capital.

Della chuckled. "Jake and I were already heading up that way in a couple of weeks. I checked with Billie, and she can keep the store sooner, rather than later. We can leave Monday."

"How will we go?"

"I'll drive us up there. Now that I traded in my truck for a bigger vehicle, we can all fit. You can have your lovefest with Jake the whole way up."

I nearabout started crying. Having friends help you out *and* a trip to Washington, D.C. bordered on a miracle. But then I thought about what a sight that would be—me with this tray in my lap and flowerdy pillowcases behind me, bawling my eyes out. That made me start chuckling. Della looked puzzled as she stood up to leave. Then she turned and added, "I don't feel good about tricking your mother. Can you tell her what's going on?"

"No!" I said, nearly upending the tray. "Really, let me have a couple of weeks or so. They won't miss me. I need to figure more of this out before I tell them anything. They'd be so ashamed of me." She nodded and let me be.

I went back to eating my breakfast. Damn, Della was a good cook. Mama worried about germs and such, so she cooked her eggs dry, but Della's were creamy and her bacon weren't burnt to a crisp. (Mama had a thing about pork and needing to cook it so she didn't give us ptomaine poisoning or something like that beginning with a T.) Just as I was thinking about that, Della stuck her head back round the door.

"They will—*do*—miss you, but I see what you mean. You've been gone a month before. But you have to go home now and spend a weekend with them. And kiss them goodbye!"

I was dreading that weekend with the folks, so I ate real slow (something I never did). I dawdled over getting dressed, too. It was well after noon when Della practically pushed me out the door.

Chapter 4

"I don't know about you," Della said, jerking me back from a doze, "but I could use a cup of coffee."

We'd started our trip early Monday morning. I'd told Mama that Della was driving me to the bus station, so I didn't have to walk in the rain. (Sure was glad to see the skies open up like they did just before breakfast.) I could tell she believed me, which kinda hurt, but it was better than telling her the truth. I was so pumped about our road trip, I worried Mama would notice how happy I was. (As much as I liked school, I wasn't usually *that* excited about going back.) But she had her dishes to do, which she was itching to get to. She hugged and kissed me and waved goodbye, ready to get on with her day. Daddy'd already gone off somewhere.

I sat in the front of the Jeep with Della, and Jake stood behind us on the flattened backseat that made it more like a truck bed. He put his paws on the console and stared out the windshield, as steadfast as a hood ornament. At first, we just rolled along, not talking about much of anything. We both needed time to wake up. Then the usual questions started: How's the store doing? How's school? What have you learned lately?

Oncet we'd finished with the easy stuff, we both fell silent again, neither of us ready to talk about why I'd been kicked out of school. I just wanted to enjoy the fact that I was getting out of North Carolina. Twenty year old, and I'd never been out of the blamed state. You'd think that excitement would have me wired, but something about the hum of the tires on the road was like a lullaby.

We'd only been on the road an hour or so when Della suggested that cup of coffee. When we stopped at the next gas station with a café, I got out and rolled my back, already stiff from sitting in her Jeep. I'd've said we did the usual things people did on road trips, but that was the first one I'd ever taken. I bought us each a coffee, and though it looked as though it'd been in the pot since last week, it tasted good. And did the trick.

For a while, we wound through scenery that looked pretty much like back home. Tall mountains, blanketed with the same kinds of trees we had in Laurel Falls, cast long shadows over the houses and buildings hugging the highway. We were in the middle of October, and the hardwoods had started to change into their fall colors. They weren't at their peak yet, which was good, because the roads would've been snarled with leaf lookers.

With each mile we traveled away from my troubles, I felt happier. Lately, I'd taken to singing more, inspired by the music I studied at school. And all the pickup bands that sprang up in different rooms. Some of the folks liked my voice and asked me to chime in. In the Jeep, I started singing to myself.

We met, loved and parted
I thought the world of you
You left me broken hearted

24

To me you proved un-true

Dark and stormy weather
It still inclines to rain
The clouds hang over center
My love's gone away on a train

"That's a sad song. What's it called?" Della asked.

It wasn't till she spoke that I realized I hadn't been singing to myself, after all. "'Dark and Stormy Weather,'" I answered. She nodded like she knew that one. Or maybe just approved of my singing.

"Where'd you learn that song?"

"I'd heard it my whole life, but at school, I took some music courses. They teach all kinds of stuff—from English country dance music to old timey mountain music. I learned the bass fiddle, mostly because I was the tallest kid at the school."

"Why's this the first time I've heard you mention your music training? If you hadn't started singing to yourself, I still wouldn't know."

"Because I'm not very good."

"You will be with a little more practice."

"But I can't practice now."

"Oh yeah, there's that. Well, we'll get to work on that. You'll be back at school by the new year. And besides, you *can* practice anytime. Like right now."

But I didn't feel like it anymore. Just thinking about what I was missing at school bummed me out.

By late morning, we'd reached Virginia. When I saw that "Welcome to Virginia" sign, my heart started pounding. Abit Bradshaw was getting out of Dodge and making his move. A little farther down the road, I saw a road sign for Mount Rogers. Something triggered in my mind. "Wild Ponies!" I blurted out.

"What? The Rolling Stones song?" Della asked. I musta looked blank because she added, "It's called 'Wild Horses.'"

"Not that. We're coming up on a park not too far away that has wild ponies I've read about. I'd love to see them for real." My newfound freedom was making my mind race with possibilities.

"We need to get to D.C. before it's real late. I hate driving in the dark."

"But aren't you the one always saying 'carpe diem'?"

I felt her foot let up off the gas for a moment and got my hopes up. But then she put it down harder than ever. "I'm carpe dieming all I can to get you to D.C. to meet with Alex. You can explore your wanderlust there."

I quit thinking about them ponies oncet we got north enough that the mountains stepped back and made way for the Shenandoah River, creating a valley the likes of which I'd never seen. It felt like Moses parting the Red Sea, at least the way the pictures looked at Sunday school. My throat tightened and my eyes burned. I was glad Della seemed lost in thought so I could turn my head and wipe my eyes. Jake helped, too. He liked them salty treats.

As we rode along, the silence became more natural. Even Jake had given up his post, passed out on his rug in the back. When we did say somethin', we talked about the darnedest things. Like how it's impossible *not* to stare at strangers along the roadside.

Della had gotten off the interstate and pulled on to U.S. Highway 11. (She said the sameness of the interstate was killing her—or would kill us both if she fell asleep at the wheel.) That was when I noticed a fellow walking on the other side of the highway, and I couldn't *not* look at him. It was the kinda thing you only thought about when you had time on your hands. I asked Della if she did the same thing. She chuckled and said yes, now that I'd mentioned it. We talked about how odd that was—we didn't know that person, he didn't even look all that interesting, but we locked eyes with him when he looked at us, too. And then he was gone.

"Why do you think that is, Della? I don't know a living soul here in wherever-the-hell-we-are Virginia, but I checked him out as though he coulda been my long-lost friend."

"I don't know, honey. It's just human nature. Maybe because everyone is special."

I didn't say anything for a while. I wasn't sure what she was getting at. Then I said, "I'd stare at a dog, if he was hoofing along the highway."

"Well, I've yet to meet a dog that wasn't special. Right, Jake?" She stretched to pat Jake when she said that. He lifted his head, but went right back to sleep.

"Okay, what about all them fine looking trees? We don't stare at all of them as we pass 'em by."

"Speak for yourself!" I laughed, because I knew she was kidding. We both hugged trees from time to time, but even as little driving as I'd done, I knew you couldn't look at every tree or you'd have a wreck. I wasn't sure whether this was important or just crazy been-in-the-car-a-long-time talk. But I liked what she said about everyone being special.

We let some time go by before we spoke again. In the quiet, I started thinking about the mess I was in, and a wave of fear took over. A ways down the road, Della musta noticed. "What's up, Abit? Or maybe I should ask what's got you down? At this moment, I mean."

"I'm sick about what just happened at school. I haven't been able to talk to anyone about this, and it's killing me inside. I was doing good there. And you know how after a couple of years, they extended my scholarship and asked me to mentor some of the younger kids? Man, I loved that. I knew how the kids felt—stupid, despised, bullied—and I got to help them, which helped me. I keep seeing how a couple of them—Andy and Jasper—were crying when I had to pack up my room and leave. I wasn't allowed to tell them why, just that I'd been called back home."

I saw Della struggling to look hopeful for me, but I couldn't imagine how even her and Alex could solve this one. Besides, there were things I couldn't tell her. I chewed on that, and after a while, I started humming, then full-out singing again.

Let us pause in life's pleasures and count its many tears
While we all sup sorrow with the poor.
There's a song that will linger forever in our ears,
Oh, hard times, come again no more.

'Tis the song, the sigh of the weary.
Hard times, hard times, come again no more.
Many days you have lingered around my cabin door.
Oh, hard times, come again no more.

I liked belting songs like that; it helped let stuff out. Della asked me to sing some more, so I started anothern. Before I got very far, she interrupted. "Hey, isn't that the Allman Brothers?"

"Yeah, 'Trouble No More,'" I said. "What's wrong?"

"Nothing," she said. "You just had me thinking old timey music and surprised me."

"Yeah, but 'Hard Times' is Stephen Foster—from the Civil War, not old timey." She raised her eyebrow, impressed-like. "Though it sure fits life in Laurel Falls," I added.

She nodded and looked about as sad as I felt at that moment. "You've got a theme going there, Mister: 'Dark and Stormy Weather.' 'Hard Times.' 'Trouble No More.'" She squeezed my shoulder. "Don't worry, honey. We're going to fix this."

Chapter 5

As we wound our way north, I kept noticing how fine the crops looked, even this late in the season. I figured the soil had to be richer and the valley sunnier than back home. And I'd never seen so many cows and cattle in one place.

We stopped kinda late for midday dinner at a truck stop just off the highway. Della picked at her food, but I plowed into mine. The country-fried steak tasted a lot like Mama's, and I'd never had mashed potatoes I didn't like, even with lumps. But the staff in there acted all grumpy-like. Before Della paid the bill, I went into the store next door and asked the guy to help me find the Kleenex, and you would've thought I'd asked him to change a tire—in the rain. When I got back to the table, Della had settled up. "You know," I told her as she gathered her belongings, "I find most people in stores and cafés aren't as nice as you are to your customers."

"Ya think?" she said, not mean but with an edge.

I knew a thing or two about customer service since Daddy had owned the store before Della bought it four year ago. He wasn't real nice round the house, but he did treat his customers pretty good. And when Della gave me a job stocking the shelves, I'd hear how she talked to each of them, valuing them and their business, in that order.

From all that, I'd come to understand how hard it was to be kind to customers eight hours a day, and how, sad to say, a lot of the folks didn't seem to notice. Though they'd

30

definitely have complained if they *didn't* get it, so I supposed their silence was a strange kind of appreciation.

"Thing is, Abit, that's probably true whether you're in a store or somewhere else. I believe people are basically good, but too many don't show it till they're called on to do so, like in an emergency or other times of need. I don't know why. Seems to me it means more, *my* life means more, when I make the effort. And there are some good folks who try to ease life's burdens every day. Like Cleva and … well, like Cleva."

"Yeah, I always figured life's hard enough without everybody being cross with one anothern."

"Listen to us," she said, slapping the table, "back a few miles, we were extolling the virtues of everyone being special, and now I make them all sound like Simon Legree."

I'd heard her use that expression before, so I knew what she was talking about. "Yeah, maybe everyone is special, like you just said, but they forget."

We took Jake out for a whiz on a forgotten patch of weeds and gravel. He seemed delighted with it. Musta been the smells. After we settled back into a steady drive, we started talking about what happened at school. Friday night, I'd just gotten started with the basics. I was ready to fill her in on how the Ledbetters had wormed their way into our hearts. We *wanted* to help them. I couldn't help but wonder how that got me in so much trouble.

I told her how we felt so damned sad that such a nice woman was dying, and she was only round 50 year old. "She had to wear them adult diapers, and she'd wince in pain, and it just cut right through you," I added. "Some folks were against our helping them so much, but they were always against everything, so we didn't pay them much mind.

"Mama Mae and Clayne and Clarice were there for just over four months, with Mae wincing more and more as she walked. I was getting scared that she was gonna leave us real soon, and then they did. All three of them were just gone one day. Before they left, they stole a bunch of stuff from the school. That was in addition to what they'd already taken in cash from all of us—asking for help with her medical bills and to pay for groceries and meals at the school. I'd been a big advocate of theirs, so people started blaming me and a few others for falling for 'them con artists.' Because that's what they were. More than likely, Mama Mae weren't dying—we found a big bag of diapers at the cottage, like she didn't need them no more. They'd just been a prop."

"They really preyed on your good intentions, Abit."

"Oh, I don't think that was the case. We never saw them go to church or anything like that."

Della chuckled and explained what she'd said. I had to laugh at myself, too. "I can imagine how much you wanted to help," she said. "And from what you've told me, how lonely you felt at times. You can be around a lot of people and still feel lonely, I know. When we're vulnerable like that, it's easy to be swayed."

"Yeah, they acted like I was special. Which felt good, because to tell you the truth, I feel like the odd one out most of the time. I'm in a place where I can't go back to my old life, but I don't know how to live whatever's next. And I hadn't been round a lot of death, at least not with people or animals I was close to. Daddy's beagles were about it. My grandparents had all passed by the time I was ten, and before that, we didn't visit them much."

"I did a story on con artists," Della said. "They're calculating—brilliant, even. They know that people want to feel needed, and they count on how predictable their marks are."

"Oh, great. Now on top of all my other bad qualities, I'm predictable." Della frowned and stopped talking. "OK, I'm sorry I interrupted," I quickly added.

"The interruption wasn't the problem, Abit. I hate it when you talk about yourself that way. And to me, your biggest fan."

I could tell she was kinda upset, but then we looked at each other and started laughing. We'd had these talks before about the way I go on like that, so it wasn't new territory. Easy to move past. "Sorry, I guess I'm just a no count," I said. She hit my arm like you do when you're playing around.

"This story I worked on, that con worked in a corporate environment, where, frankly, a lot of cons were going down, only they were seen as legit."

"How's that?"

"The greed was sanctioned. Corporate America. Get what you can out of people to make the bottom line look good. The con, or grifter, as they prefer to be called (she sounded real sarcastic and made a face that went along with that), just takes it to a new level—and makes sure plenty of the graft lines his pockets. The fact that he was making money for the company made them all look the other way. He preyed on their avarice—and to be fair, their compassion and human kindness, since he, too, shared a sob story about his health."

I felt better that I wasn't the only idiot to fall for such a trick. But that didn't last long after Della asked, "How did she get your personal info? Like your savings account number?"

That took me back to the week before I got thrown out, before everything blew up. I was walking along the nature trail that ran from my room to the main office at school, just minding my own business, thinking about what was for lunch. Next thing I knew, someone ran up behind me and threw both hands over my eyes.

"Guess who!"

Even with my eyes closed, I knew it was Clarice. She was pressing right against my back, you know, and that plus her voice, well, I knew it weren't no boy. But I didn't want to ruin her game, so I named a few girls at the school. Finally, I asked, "Clarice?"

"You knew all along, didn't you, V.J.? You just wanted to feel my breasts against your back for longer." She laughed and pinched my cheek, which I knew was burning red. "I don't know why you're so shy that way," she added.

"Well, I don't know you all that well." I knew I sounded like somebody at Mama's church, but I *didn't* know her that well. And I was embarrassed, her talking about breasts out in broad daylight. She musta read my mind, because she asked if we could go to my room, which was nearby in the Barn House. (Not hard to figure it was oncet a barn, which gave it some great features like tall ceilings in every room and a good feeling, not quite a smell but something deeper that soothed me to sleep most nights. I could almost hear the cows lowing and the horses nickering.)

"I don't think that'd be a good idea. We're not supposed to have guests in our rooms."

She sidled up next to me and whispered in my ear, "Guests or girls?"

I tried to answer but the words came out more like a croak. I cleared my throat to try to cover. As it turned out, her being so pretty—and persistent—won me over. We walked together to the Barn House without saying a lot and climbed the steps to my third-story room. I opened the door and motioned for her to head on in. When I closed the door and turned round, not sure what to do next, she surprised me.

"Could you get me some coffee? I saw a coffee pot on the first floor." I musta looked confused—I *was*—so she added, "I'm sorry, I should've asked for it earlier, but it wasn't until we climbed all those steps that I realized how tired I am."

"Well, sure. I'll be right back," I said. "I've got a good book there on bluegrass, if you need something to read."

"That's not what I'm needing," she said, sitting on my bed and kinda lying back.

As I headed for the stairs, I remembered I didn't know how she took her coffee, so I poked my head back in the room. "How d'you take it?" I asked. That was when I noticed she was looking at things on my desk.

"Take what?" she said, dropping something.

"Your coffee."

She smiled real sweet-like. "Now, see—I told you I needed a pick-me-up! I like cream and one sugar."

When I got back with the coffee, she was standing by the window, looking out. I hoped no one saw her there. She turned and smiled again, before taking a few sips from the mug. "This sure is a nice room you have, especially compared to the dark ole Gate House."

"Yeah, I like it just fine. I used to be in a different room, and it was dark, like you said about your home. They didn't build these old buildings with a lot of windows. Eva told me that was typical of the Arts and Crafts style that …"

"Oh, who wants to talk about old buildings?" she said, and just like that, she kissed me on the cheek, put the mug down, and said she had to run along.

Man, that was so weird. Of course, I didn't want to tell Della all that, so I just told her Clarice had tricked me into leaving her alone in my room.

"So that's likely when she got your bank and other personal information, but how did *that* get you kicked out of school?" Della asked.

"I thought about nothing else on my bus trip home. I figured since the banker at that bank in Boone, where I'd moved my account oncet I started school, is on the board at The Hicks, he musta told the director about my windfall. Apparently a teller had reported a girl for putting $2,000 *into my* savings account."

"The teller was a teller, eh?" Della loved them wordplays, from her days of writing headlines, but I didn't feel like playing. She noticed. "Sorry, Abit. Occupational hazard. So, what did you tell them—the director and banker—after they'd accused you?"

"Just that I had no idea where that money came from, but it had to be from them. The description of the girl fit Clarice. I don't know why the Ledbetters singled me out, though I believe Clarice was trying to help me—payback

for the money I'd given and all the other stuff I'd done for them. We were getting to be close friends. I think her intentions were good. I'm not sure if Mama Mae and Clayne even knew she did that."

Della's eyebrows kinda furrowed, then she patted my arm in a kindly way. "Sounds like you've been through a lot, Abit. Let's finish this when we see Alex. No point in your having to tell the whole story all over again."

I think she believed me, which was such a fine thing I felt my eyes well up again. A look out the Jeep window at some Jersey cows grazing quieted me down, reminding me of those beautiful afternoons at the school. Like the time I got to see the birth of a baby calf. Me and Clarice were hanging out on the mountain slope while I watched over the cows. We were in the pasture where the cows in the family way stayed till their babies were born. I heard some low mooing—moaning, really—and looked over to see that baby calf just slip right out of its mama. I'd been in the country all my life, but I'd never seen a calf born, or anything, really, other than puppies. The mother started licking her baby right away, getting off all the blood and stuff. I took Clarice's hand and walked over closer, but not too close. I didn't want to scare the mother and baby.

"Oh, that is *so* gross," Clarice said.

"Huh?"

"That," she said, pointing at what the cow was doing.

All I could think was how getting to witness something like that made me a better person and the world a better place. It was hard to explain, but it did. Not just that the calf was born, but that the mother loved it, licked it, and guided it into its new life. I didn't say that, though. I didn't want to piss off Clarice, so I just kept watching. She kinda pouted and went back to the rocks where we usually sat.

After a few minutes, that baby got up on wobbly legs, looked round as if to say, "Hello, world," and lumbered over to its mama's sack. She gave it a couple of good whacks and started suckling. Just like that, in a matter of minutes of being born. I'd seen calves in the field whack their mamas like that, and I thought it looked painful. When I asked

Mama, she told me that was to get the milk to come down. She didn't seem to feel any sympathetic pains, so I figured why should I?

"You're ignoring me!" Clarice said in a whiny voice. I was afraid she'd leave, and I was enjoying having her hang out with me, so I turned away, though I kept checking on that baby from time to time. It was walking round the pasture, not far from its mama, as though it knew exactly what to do.

"What do you want to do?" I asked.

"What do you think?"

I thought she was foolin' with me, so I asked, "Go to the movies? Play a game?"

"Yeah, let's play a game," she said and leaned over and kissed me like I'd never been kissed before. That set off a neon sign in my head flashing MORE, MORE, MORE.

Chapter 6

"Watcha thinking about over there?" Della said, jolting me outta my daydream.

"Oh, er, nothing much." I felt my face flush, but when I snuck a look, she had her eyes on the road.

"I need more coffee and maybe a snack. Dinner will be late," she said.

I kinda wished I could've kept daydreaming, but I was ready for a break, too. I told Della sure thing, but while she searched for a place to stop, I couldn't resist finishing up that memory.

Not long after a bunch more kisses, Clarice got up to leave. I reached for her, but she pulled away. At first I was in a daze. Those kisses really screwed up my thinking. When I stood up, she gave me a little hug and said she had to go.

"Why? We just got started," I asked.

"Mama Mae and Clayne expect me home now." She looked so sad as I brushed the hair out of her eyes. "Please be my friend," she whispered. "They don't understand me. They're always trying to make me do this or that. I'm different from them. I love them, but I can't just be their puppet."

"Of course not," I said, as though I knew what I was talking about. I put my arm round her and hugged. "Maybe you could stay a little longer and we could talk about it." I was trying anything.

She gave me another sad smile and said, "No, they're waiting. It's like they've got a stopwatch, allowing me out of my cage for an exact amount of time." Then she headed down the hill. I watched for her to turn and wave, but she never did.

"Abit!" Della called out, like she'd been trying to get my attention. "I don't know what's going on in that head of yours, but it's time to tie on the feedbag. I found a good place."

We stopped at the Skyline Diner, a place Della remembered from when she did a story on the town of Woodstock, Virginia—something about it being *the other* Woodstock. When I saw the waitress bringing folks their suppers, I knew I wanted some of the biscuits—a good three inches high. A couple of those plus some sausage gravy, and I was happy. Della got a biscuit with butter and honey. And we both guzzled more coffee. We even got a cup for the road.

I was good and sick of the car by then, but it wasn't long before we turned off I-81 onto I-66 to head toward D.C. Traffic was heavy going into town, but the cars coming out of town were at a standstill. Della explained about rush hour. All in all, I was glad I'd never have to drive in that!

I liked the way the sun stayed out a lot longer in that valley, not hiding behind mountains come three or four o'clock of an evening. Even so, the sun was getting low, and before long, it was just orange streaks on the horizon.

41

LYNDA McDANIEL

I wasn't sure why, but I felt this happiness come over me. Something about being in the car while it was getting dark outside, the dashboard lit up like a spaceship control panel, made me feel safe. And excited about being away from home with Della and Jake, heading somewhere I'd never been before.

That got me thinking about how many people don't seem happy, including folks who claim to be good Christians. Della and I'd already seen that on the trip—like at cafés and gas stations where "Jesus loves you" bumper stickers were plastered all over, even the bathrooms, but the people working there hadn't gotten the message. At our last stop, good as the food was, the cashier was curt when Della told her how much we enjoyed our meal. Maybe her husband had just left her, or her dog had been run over, but I couldn't help feeling sad that so many contrary people were wasting their lives—and my time.

"It's like all those so-called Christians have forgotten completely about Matthew 25," I said.

"Oookay," Della said, "and which left field is that coming out of?"

I laughed. It was funny how you'd think you'd been having a conversation, but it was all inside your own head—until you blurted something out. "I was just thinking about all the Christians I was raised round who treated me bad or who were unfriendly in your store—or worse. They go strutting round like their shit don't stink, but what about Matthew 25? I didn't take to church the way Mama wanted me to, but that one from the Bible really stuck with me."

"And which one is that, Abit?"

"Whatever you do for the least of these, you do for me. I think I remembered that one because it made me feel like I belonged. That Jesus was talking about me, to me. But really, he wasn't just talking about poor people or sick people or people like me, but *everybody*. Whatever you do to *anyone*, you do to him. That's how I take it. If you treat someone like shit, you better think twicet because it's like treating Jesus that a-way."

"Now wouldn't that make a good sermon title at your mother's church at the VFW? Can't you just see that on one of those sermon billboards we're always driving by?"

"Yeah, they'd really love my take on that. But you know, without the swear words, it *is* a damned good message. It's what I believe. And that's how I got myself into all of this."

"How's that?"

"Well, I was trying to be nice to people who were in trouble, sick and dying, or sad about a loved one who was."

"That wasn't the problem, Abit. The problem was they didn't deserve your favors. And you couldn't have known that. Their con was that plausible."

Maybe she was right, but my life was still a mess.

I musta dozed off, because next thing I knew, I heard Della saying, "Wake up, Abit. We're crossing the Teddy Roosevelt Bridge now, and I want you to get the best first impression of D.C." A little later, she added, "We're now on Constitution Avenue."

43

I'd never seen so many lights, even at Christmastime. Everywhere—bridges, buildings, streets. Some were regular lights and some gave off a glow that stained the buildings and streets orange, making everything even more magical. As we made our way along that avenue, a roar of excitement took hold of me, my heart racing as we drove deeper into the city where the Washington Monument pointed toward heaven.

Della turned on to a road and told me we were heading up Connecticut Avenue. "I know you're sick of being in the car, but this is such a special time, and I want you to get the best first impression," she said.

"I'm not the least bit sick of the car at the moment," I told her. We were riding in and out of tunnels, old houses with curlicue decorations and tower-like rooms appearing at the other end, lining up one after the other, like fancy-dressed women touching shoulders at a parade. Della'd talked a lot about this place, and I'd watched stuff on TV, but I could see that the images I'd formed in my mind's eye were tiny compared to the grand size of it all.

"This is Cleveland Park," she said after a while, "where I grew up."

"Did you go to that big theater?" I asked as we passed the Uptown, which looked about twenty times the size of the Hen Theater back home. I couldn't be sure, but I was pretty certain my jaw was hanging open 'cause I could feel the chilly night air on my tongue.

"You betcha," was all she said. I could tell she was enjoying herself, thinking about her past and the things she'd done when she lived here. Her reaction was about exact opposite of how I'd feel reliving my early years. At some point, she turned the Jeep round, and we went back the way we came. Which was okay, because I saw things from a different view. I got a good glimpse of the National Zoo, somewhere I hoped we'd get to come back to.

"We're heading to Georgetown, now, where Alex lives, at least some of the time. It's where I used to live."

"Yeah, so how's that going? Him living here sometimes and back home the rest of the time?"

"It's going good, Abit. I'm real happy to have him with me in Laurel Falls. But you know, sometimes I'm just as happy to see him head up the road for a while. I think we've found our rhythm."

Back in the day, that would've surprised me. I wouldn't have thought those two could ever make peace with the past. But after a few years at The Hicks, I could imagine just about anything. Even so, what I saw next blew me away.

Chapter 7

WELCOME MR. BRADSHAW!

So said the banner draped between two trees in the yard Della parked in front of.

"Is this it?" I asked, looking at the brick house with its red door and brass lanterns on each side.

"Now what would give you that idea?" Della said, smiling and ruffling my hair like she used to. I was six foot two inches now, so the only reason she could reach the top of my head was because I was stuck in the Jeep, my seatbelt jammed against Jake's wiggling body. I opened my door, and he jumped over me, running straight to the front door. I saw Alex standing there waving, then bending down to rub Jake all over. Man, what a sight. I ran up there, too, for my bear hug.

"You're looking good, Abit." He held me back, like an aunt or grandmother does right before she says something about how much you've grown. He didn't say that, but I knew he was thinking it. Instead, he said, "You are one handsome fellow, Abit, er, V.J. Is that what you prefer these days? I wasn't sure, so that's why the banner is so formal."

I laughed. I hadn't ever been called Mr. Bradshaw, but it had a nice ring to it. I told him that at school, and such, I preferred V.J. with people who'd met me more recent-like. "But when you and Della call me Abit," I added, "I kinda like it." He shook his head, like he thought I was little crazy, then went inside and motioned for me to follow.

His house could've been in a magazine—not the stuffy kind but the really cool ones. The furniture was all comfortable looking and the rooms were painted nice colors like pale blue in the living room and yellow in the kitchen. Mama thought color was the devil's work, or at least she used to. She was getting better about stuff like that. But still, the idea of her up on a ladder painting a room yellow just made me laugh. Alex musta seen me start to smile funny, because he asked, "What's up? Don't you like my sense of design?" But he was just kidding, and I didn't make a fuss to straighten things out. I didn't need to with him.

"It's grand," I said as I plopped down on the overstuffed sofa. I'd been riding in the car forever, but it looked so comfy, I just had to try it.

The kitchen was the best room in the house. I spent a fair amount of time in the school's kitchen—chopping stuff and running that awful hot dishwasher—and even that big kitchen didn't seem as well-stocked as this one. A big pot of vegetable soup was simmering on the stove, and Alex had made a skillet of cornbread, 'specially for me, I'd've bet. We sat round a handmade oak table and ate—again! (Neither me or Della wanted to tell Alex we'd loaded up on biscuits in Woodstock.)

It took every bit of politeness I could muster not to crawl under that table and look at the joinery and finer details. I took a couple of woodworking classes at school, and if they ever let me back in, I planned to take more.

LYNDA McDANIEL

"So, what brings you up here?" Alex asked.

"Della," I answered with a mouth full of cornbread. They both started laughing, though I hadn't meant to be funny. I realized then he was just opening up the conversation. "Well, she thought I might like a change of scenery, and that maybe you could help me figure out what went wrong—and how to fix it."

I brought him up to date with what Della and I'd talked about on the drive. Then I added some rumors I'd heard. "That last day, when I was packing up, Eva the cook—and believe me, those two cooks didn't miss a thing, though sometimes they stretched the truth to make it juicier—told me she'd heard that the school had been fleeced for about $20,000, which was the down payment old man Henson, the director, had put on some land near the school that was supposed to have been Mama Mae's family home. Seems they couldn't live there because the estate was in testing, and ..."

"Intestate," Alex interrupted.

"Oh, yeah, that's what Eva called it. Anyways, Mama Mae said she could sell it and, after sharing it with other family members, get some money for her medical bills. Eva said Henson was buying that land for an experimental farm for the school. It weren't right next to the school, but close enough they could teach and try growing different things on the land. But then she made a whoever-believes-that-is-a-fool face and added that he was likely setting up his family on a nice piece of property away from all the headaches of the school."

"Okay, I'll look into that," Alex said. "But did Henson say why he was expelling you, Abit?"

"Not really. He and that banker said they didn't want to call the cops, but they would if I didn't leave without making a fuss. And, of course, they made me give back the money that had been stashed in my account. Which I'd've done even if they hadn't asked, for heaven's sake."

I went on about how this had all happened one morning, while most of the other students were in class. I did like they said and packed up my room—Andy and Jasper didn't have classes just then, so that was why they were standing nearby, crying. I stored my bags in the Barn House, except for my usual overnight bag. I told them I'd be back for my stuff, but I didn't know when I'd feel like showing my face there again. I was in shock, so it wasn't hard to behave the way they'd wanted. But as I rode the bus toward home, I got madder and madder. "That was when I got off and started walking. Besides, I wanted to arrive home in the dark, so Mama and Daddy wouldn't see me coming. By the time we got here, Alex, I've worked out some of my anger, but just retelling it makes me mad all over again."

They both sat quiet-like, taking it all in. I was hoping their wheels were turning on how to help me out. The way they'd teamed up to find Lucy Sanchez's killer in 1985, the same year Della and I became such good friends. Sheriff Brower wouldn't get off his big butt and do anything, but they wouldn't let that poor girl die without finding out who'd wronged her.

After a while, I got kinda nervous about so much silence and added, "You wouldn't believe how good these folks were—are." Alex nodded in a way that let me know he mighta been taken a time or two by con artists (or at least written about them). "I mean Mama Mae wore them diapers for people who couldn't make it to the bathroom on time. You could see them bunching up in the back of her pants. On my bus trip home, though, I recalled one time seeing her coming out of the bathroom at the Gate House. I'd stopped by to see if Clarice wanted to go to the Fall Festival at the school—and Mama Mae looked real nervous. I was afraid I'd barged in at a bad time, making me the nervous one, so I started chattering about the festival. 'It's a lot of fun if you want to join us. It's got art and crafts and lots of music,' I told her. She seemed caught off guard and turned to leave the room, calling out for Clarice. That's when I noticed she didn't have them bunches back there. I know because her sickness had caught my attention; I worried for her health, always checking to see if she might be feeling better. She turned back round and looked really flustered and told me to go. I was so embarrassed I left without saying another word. It wasn't until I got to the festival that I realized she'd looked different—thinner and healthier. Looking back, I figure she didn't have on her pale makeup or diapers. But at the time, stupid me, I just felt happy that maybe she was getting over what ailed her."

"Nothing stupid about that," Alex said. "That's just human decency shining through. Something she'd lost somewhere along the way."

I nodded, grateful he understood. "So they played us like a fiddle. Which, by the way, I've learned to play. The big bass fiddle."

Della and Alex looked at each other, kinda proud-like. "That school has opened up a lot more than books for you," Alex said, then motioned for me to go on.

"I've thought about it over and over, and I can't figure out why they set me up. I was their friend. And why'd they want to make me look bad by *giving* me money."

"For starters, they were really good at knowing exactly what you—and everyone else involved—wanted, and playing to that," Alex said. "Con artists are some of the most creative people I've ever met. I'll tell you more about some of them tomorrow."

I hadn't told them the half of it, but it was getting late, and I was tired of talking. Besides, they didn't need to know *every* detail. I did mention briefly what I'd already told Della—that Clarice musta gotten my savings account number one of those times she was hanging out in my room. "I had nearly $2,600 in there of my own money, thanks to you, Della, hiring me to work at the store. It's possible Clayne and Mama Mae put Clarice up to it to make me look guilty and take the rap—or maybe Clarice felt bad for all the trouble they'd caused. Either way, I returned the money to the bank—though I don't know what happened to it after that. And then they still wouldn't let me into my savings account. My own money! 'Assets frozen until further investigation,' they told me."

"I'm sorry, Abit, that you got ripped off on so many levels—the school, the bank, that Mae character, and Clarice."

"Oh, I still think they forced Clarice to do what she did. She really liked me, I could tell." I'd already decided not to mention the kisses. When they looked unconvinced, I added, "Really, if you'd seen her and how nice she was, way nicer than Mae or Clayne."

"So it's clear this wasn't the first time they'd pulled their con act," Della said, changing the subject.

"Oh, they knew what they were doing, all right. Which makes me wonder who they're scamming right now."

"That's what we're going to find out," Alex said. He and Della stood up and started clearing the table. I offered to help, but they told me to stay put, they'd get this round. I felt a kick of hope revive me after that long car trip. I knew Alex was going to do his thing.

That night, I lay awake a long time in Alex's guestroom. I liked the feel of the crisp navy-striped cotton sheets and a blue cotton blanket. (I couldn't imagine getting breakfast in bed there!) I thought I'd fall right to sleep, but I still felt like I was moving down the highway. I stared at the ceiling for the longest time, thinking about school and how much I'd learned over the past four years. My favorite classes were woodworking and, believe it or not, English. And I'd improved my carving (well, really, all I'd ever done before was whittling) by watching some of the more famous carvers at the school. One in particular, Jack Harper, was real nice to me, and, boy, could he ever carve those crèche figures. You halfway expected to hear the little baby Jesus start crying in his tiny manger.

All kinds of people showed up at the school—rich and poor, creatives and wannabes, free-spirits and up-tights. The folks who came for a week or two were always hepped up about something, and were usually eager to share it with anyone they could rope into listening. One woman was a nut about the stars and planets. She'd set up her telescope just behind the Barn House and look into the heavens (oohing and ahhing about how dark it was there, away from the city lights where she lived). I thought of her a lot when I looked at the sky; I'd hear her going on about gibbous moons and crescent moons and constellations. Another guy, a professor from Michigan, taught me stuff about birds I'd never heard before. He'd also set up a big telescope (in the daytime) so we could see feathers close up and look right into their eyes, if we were lucky.

But I'd be telling only half the story if I didn't mention the people who were weird, too. Not quite tethered to this earth. We figured the school attracted so many odd folks because it was listed in some hippie magazines and the like. The folks in the school's office seemed pretty good at figuring out which guests were the weirdos, and they'd put them in with us regulars to keep them kinda separate from the rest.

Like Steve Thompson, this cool guy who taught me even more than Mama had about wild edibles. We made some cattail stew and redbud syrup for ice cream. That part wasn't strange. What I had trouble with was the way Steve and his wife bragged about how good they were doing with coffee enemas. Every morning, they put coffee up their butts! He'd come running in, all happy about being "up to a quart a day!" I couldn't imagine; in fact, I didn't *want* to imagine. He didn't look all that healthy, so I figured I could skip that little self-improvement tip. (Of course, no telling how bad he might've looked if he *hadn't* taken his coffee that a-way.)

He also said to put mashed-up garlic on my feet to ward off a cold that was trying to set in. Eva thought I was crazy when I asked for a head of garlic, but I'd've tried anything to stave off a cold. So, I put petroleum jelly on my feet and a bunch of the garlic mash, just like he told me, and then covered that up with an old pair of socks. Trouble was, not only did I get the blamed cold, my feet got blisters the size of pancakes, which hurt at first and then itched like crazy when they started to heal. A couple of times in class I had to take my boots off and scratch. Between blowing my nose.

One of my favorite weirdos was Brock, who wrote to the school asking permission to lower the ceiling in his room so he had to walk round on all fours, which he explained would help him commune more with animals. (I couldn't've made stuff like that up.) Thing was, there weren't ever any animals in his room other than his fellow humans. Why didn't he just walk round in the woods or in the pastures on all fours and commune like that?

Anyways, at the time, the school needed the cash, so they said yes to him—at a pretty high price. But Brock was from old New England money (who but the rich would have time for such things?), so that wasn't a problem. I found him to be a friendly guy, and he often had us over for beers and popcorn and snacks. (None of which I'd ever seen an animal eat, except sometimes when I'd throw popcorn to Jake.) Mercifully for all of us, he did allow himself the luxury of a thick rug—the floors in Barn House were hand-hewn oak and hard as a rock—and we'd crawl in and have a good time together. I imagined it was like one of those secret clubs I'd read about.

And some of the guests said the craziest things. Like these two women who arrived when the school was holding classes in English county dance. They met on the dance floor and started chatting, and after a while, I overheard one of them say, "I just luuuu-uv your Richmond accent," and then the other woman cooed, "Well, I just luuuu-uv your Montgomery accent." I knew from books and TV that outsiders made a lot fun of the way we talked back home, but these women didn't sound all that different from us. They were better schooled than folks in Laurel Falls, but they were still Southern and said a lot of things like we did. Oh, they luuuu-uved that just fine, but when we said "of an evening" and "young'uns" and "reckon," we was just hicks in their eyes.

The staff could be as crazy as the students and guests. Not my teachers—they were real smart and, all in all, nice to us—but them cooks, Lurline and Eva, were a couple of wildcats. You didn't want to get on the wrong side of them. One day when I was helping out in the kitchen chopping vegetables, Lurline and Eva went at each other with kitchen knives, and I had to break it up. My arm got caught in the crossed knives, but it didn't need stitches. From then on, those two treated me real nice 'cause I didn't report them. I just told everyone I'd accidentally cut myself. (Yeah, sure. While I was chopping, my upper arm got in the way!)

Down the hill from the main buildings, the old blacksmith shop was run by the nicest smithy I'd ever met. I'd known a few, and they could be crotchety, probably because of all that hot, hard work. Jim and his wife, Rosie, lived in the Mill House, oncet a real mill but now a dorm for students with a smart-looking apartment next door, where they lived.

Rosie spoke real soft-like and had a gentle way about her. One day she said, "Don't be lonely. You have the whole universe inside you." That blew my mind because I didn't know anyone could tell I was so lonesome. (To be honest, I hadn't put that word to my feelings till she said that.) I told her that was a beautiful thing she'd just said, and she smiled and told me it was from her favorite roomie. I musta looked baffled because Jim was the only roommate she had, so why didn't she say his name? She picked up on that and explained who Rumi was.

I'd liked to have spent more time with Jim and Rosie, but it seemed she was always off somewhere meditating. Lots of people at the school did that, and I'd tried it, getting quiet and listening for messages about life. But I wasn't much good at it, which meant that every time I did see Rosie, I felt kinda guilty.

I did that to myself—whatever someone else was into, I thought I should be, too. I was hell-bent on bettering myself, and I paid attention to the way people I liked lived their lives. But to be honest, the idea of shutting myself off from the world sounded too much like the way I growed up. I was just getting *out* in the world, and I was loving it. Luuuu-uving it. I wanted to live this life as much as possible. Try things, eat things, do things I'd never done before. I didn't think I could ever fit all I wanted to do in one lifetime, so I couldn't see shutting myself up like that. Eventually, though, I made a sort of peace with all that. Just like there were priests and preachers doing good for the world, well, maybe Rosie was like that. In her own way, she was doing her good for the world, too. I just needed to figure out what my good was.

Chapter 8

Every time Jake did his business, I had to bend over and pick it up with a plastic bag. That was law in Georgetown. Well, actually, in all of D.C. I couldn't help but chuckle, thinking what Duane and Wilkie would think if they'd seen me picking up dog turds. But Alex told me about a study in Paris, France, that found ice cream cones outside were covered in tiny bits of dog shit, and it started to make sense. Back home, we didn't walk round much eating ice cream, but if we did, I'd bet it'd be sprinkled with specks of cow patty.

Hanging out with Della and Alex in D.C. helped me forgot my troubles. Della took me to the Washington Monument, the Jefferson Monument, and the Lincoln Memorial, where we walked round and looked up at Honest Abe. I mean, what else could you do to that man? (Lots of folks back home didn't understand that he did good things for our country, but I'd learned different at school.) And we went to the National Gallery of Art, where I saw stuff that blew my mind. Not to mention the building itself was a work of art. We didn't have time for the zoo, Della told me, but then she added the magic words: *this time.*

Alex lived on P Street, a ways from the hubbub of M Street and Connecticut Avenue. I liked hitching up Jake and walking through the small streets and looking at the grand old churches with towering steeples and well-tended gardens. (They sure put Mama's church in the VFW Hall in the shade.) I especially enjoyed walking past florists with bouquets of flowers spilling out of the store, the air perfumed for a block or more. Jake pulled on the leash when I stopped to look in the windows of the wine and fancy tableware shops. I couldn't believe anyone would pay $300 for a bottle of wine or a tablecloth that was sure to get stains on it the first time it was used, at least with me at the table.

As we walked past the plate-glass windows, I caught a glimpse of myself and realized I looked a sight in Alex's hand-me-downs. I hadn't brought many clothes with me because I'd left school with just the shirt on my back, so I was wearing high-water pants with white socks showing a good three inches. He also gave me a flannel shirt, which seemed really out of place in Georgetown, so it musta been one he wore when he came down to Laurel Falls.

When we got back from our walk, Alex was outside getting the mail as we walked up. I waved real big, and he waved back. Then he did a double-take and said, "Say, Abit, maybe we better go shopping." Alex had bought me all kinds of "cool duds" (that's what he called them) when I first met him four year ago. Man, I'd loved that, but I didn't feel right asking him to pay again, especially since I had money in a savings account, if I could ever get at it.

"I don't have any money, Alex. Like I said, they froze everything."

"Who says you have to pay? Let me take you out for some cool duds."

"Let's make it a loan, till I get my money back."

"We'll see," he said, and I just nodded because I always got kinda choked up when he was nice to me. I think he knew it, because he turned as though he suddenly needed to get inside.

Later on, I wasn't trying to eavesdrop, but it just happened Alex and Della were working together in Alex's office with the door open. I was walking by as I headed back downstairs when I heard Alex say to Della, "I called that damn director for more information on why he threw Abit out of school. I wanted a straight answer about what happened." Alex stopped, like he was trying to control himself. I could tell he was wrought up. "That son of a bitch tried talking in circles, blaming Abit for *cohorting*—his word—with those three, as if he were in on their con."

"What did you say to that?" Della asked. I could tell she was mad, too, and happy Alex was sticking up for me.

"I told him I knew he'd been swindled, too, and that if he didn't want me to go to the full board—including my editor friend who's on the board and who's in a position to run a full twenty inches on this outrageous situation—he and his banker friend had better unfreeze Abit's savings account and at least come clean with *me*."

"Did it work? And did he know your friend could never get that much space for this story?"

"Well, no and no. But I made some other calls and pieced together how Henson found out he'd been swindled. Seems he showed up at the property he'd made the down payment on and asked the farmer living there when he'd be moving out. The farmer grabbed a shotgun and said he wasn't moving, but he knew who'd better get a move on. In the end, though, it was the suspicious way Henson was acting that confirmed in my mind he was hiding something much bigger than just Abit's troubles. That's when I told him that if he threw our boy under the bus to cover his own issues ..."

"You said *our* boy," Della interrupted.

"No, I didn't."

"Did."

"Well, he *is* our boy, in a way."

I tiptoed away, afraid they'd catch me grinning like a fool.

That afternoon, Alex and I walked downtown, a little ways past where Jake and I'd gone. Alex stopped outside a shop tucked between a hotel and a restaurant called Millard's and opened the door for me to go in. "Hello, Mr. Covington," the man behind the counter called out as we walked into the dim light. It took my eyes a minute to adjust.

"Hello, Carter. I want you to meet my friend V.J. Bradshaw." A short, plump man came out from behind the counter and shook my hand. He had a tape measure round his neck, so I figured he was Alex's tailor. But as I looked round, it seemed more like a place where clothes got dumped when they'd sat in other shops too long.

"Hey, don't worry, Abit," Alex whispered. "I know it looks as though I've brought you to a bargain basement, but I find some of my favorite clothes here."

Man, this guy is spooky, I thought, reading my mind again. But as we dug in some bins and looked on the rack, I saw what he meant. I found a really cool black leather vest that with jeans made me think of Merle Haggard. And a denim jacket that wasn't far off from what I'd seen on other kids at school. Then we got the basics—including a pair of jeans that were, for oncet in my life, too long for me. That was when that tape measure came in handy; Carter took my measurements and had me hand him the jeans. He went behind a curtain, I put my high-water pants back on, and we took care of the rest of our shopping. By the time we'd finished picking out stuff, Carter was back with the jeans, just the right length. The other pair of pants we found fit perfectly.

"I'll pay you back, Alex, when we solve this mess."

"No, that won't happen."

"We're not gonna solve this mess?"

"No," he said, slapping my shoulder and chuckling. "No need to pay me back. I don't get to see enough of you these days, so we're good."

Chapter 9

"It's grand to meet you, V.J.," Nigel Steadman said as he shook my hand. "Della has told me wonderful things about you."

Della'd driven us to Dupont Circle to meet Nigel, the forger who'd looked over some handwritten notes when she was working on Lucy Sanchez's murder. She'd known Nigel from her reporter days—he was a crackerjack forger who'd had a successful career in crime until he faced either doing jail time or working with the Feds. He chose the Feds.

I'd felt antsy on the way over, wondering what it would be like to come face-to-face with a criminal, even one Della liked. But oncet I met him, all that flew out the window. Della had described Nigel to me before, and just that morning over breakfast, she'd told me to be prepared for a very proper English gentleman. Okay, the suit and tie and silky-looking vest (Della called it a waistcoat) were old-fashioned, but otherwise, that guy was cool.

His apartment looked like a museum with artwork and curios all over the place. About ten clocks on the wall in the living room (which he called his parlor) were ticking away at slightly different times. And I noticed how tidy and clean everything was, too. No dog hairs all over the velvet settee or boot marks at the front door, the way my place would've looked, if I'd had one. When Nigel invited us to take a seat, I chose the settee, not because it looked comfortable (it wasn't), but because it reminded me of my grandmother's house.

He put out some biscuits (he called them scones, but they looked like Mama's biscuits) and poured tea. There was a jar of yellow stuff that Della heaped on her biscuit, so I did, too. Man, it was all creamy and lemony and made my mouth pucker.

"So, you like the curd, do you?" Nigel asked. Something about that word *curd* didn't set well, and I kinda gagged. He laughed, like he knew what was goin' on. "That's lemon curd. The name isn't nearly as appealing as the taste, is it?"

I nodded with a mouthful. We drank our tea, and they chatted about old times and stories Della had worked on while a reporter in D.C. I had another biscuit, this time without the lemon stuff. The top was crisp and slightly sugary, which I slathered with more butter. I took a big bite just as Della came round to thanking him again for his help with the fake suicide note made to look like Lucy'd killed herself. We'd worked together on that, and it felt good when they drew me back into the conversation.

"I understand you played a big role in solving that case, V.J." Nigel said.

Oncet I'd swallowed the last of my biscuit, I said, "Well, I wouldn't say a big role, but I was glad to help. That was a real sad time."

We sat quiet for a while after that, thinking about how that story wasn't just some adventure we'd all been on but a tragedy for many folks. Then Nigel cleared his throat and said, "Well, I hear you're embroiled in a new kerfuffle."

I looked at Della who mouthed *problem*. "Oh, yes, sir. I'm knee-deep in a kerfuffle." They both laughed, but not mean-like.

"Tell me more."

So I ran through the story about school and how I loved it there, but some con artists took that away from me. I saw Nigel wince when I said "con artists," probably remembering how his forgeries had taken a lot of money from a lot of people. He seemed to have turned over a new leaf, though, so I was happy to give him the benefit of the doubt. I told him Alex and Della were working to help us find them.

"Do you have any pictures of them?" he asked.

"No. And now that you mention it, they'd slip away whenever anyone had a camera out. Some of the students came only for a week or two, and they were always running round taking pictures to capture memories. It's a beautiful place. You should come visit sometime."

"Thank you, V.J., for that kind invitation. I hope I can someday. So, can you describe these scoundrels? In detail, I mean."

"Uh, yeah. I believe they're tattooed on my brain, after what they did to me. Though I've got to say, I'm pretty sure Clarice, the daughter, was roped into the swindle. She was really nice to me."

"I'm glad to hear that," he said. "But one way or the other, she's part of this gang of three, and I'm thinking I might be able to help you with that."

Della looked confused, and I figured I did, too. "But they didn't forge anything. They just stole it out right!" I said without thinking, though he didn't seem to take offense.

"Well, the reason I ask is I'm a bit of an artist, and not just at forgery," he said, sweeping his arm round the room. He got up and added, "Excuse me a minute," before heading down the hallway.

That's when I paid more attention to all the paintings, one at a time rather than the overall look of the room. Della did, too, and got up close to one in particular. "Wow! I've always loved this painting, and I had no idea Nigel painted it. I honestly thought it was something he bought with his loot."

"Loot, eh?" Nigel said, coming back in the room with a big wooden box. "I'm glad you think it would cost a lot," he added, smiling at her. He blew some dust off the box and held it up for us to see.

"Why do you have an Identi-Kit?" Della asked.

"Oh, my. It's a long story, but basically, I knew I wanted to create art, but I needed to make a living. I got involved with some nefarious characters, as you know, and that's when I turned my skills to forgery. I was well into my, uh, craft, when I was pulled in by the cops, and as I waited, handcuffed to a detective's desk, the man sitting at the next desk was describing a culprit to a police artist, who was using one of these. I was so intrigued, I almost forgot I was in trouble!" He chuckled, as though remembering something wonderful. I guessed it was, in a way. "So after my attorney got me off, I ordered one of these," he added, holding up the wooden box again.

He started pulling out all kinds of cards—line drawings on clear, plasticky sheets with all kinds of noses and eyes and chins and hairdos and head shapes. It seemed kinda out of date, but I still wanted to see how it worked.

First, he asked me a bunch of questions about their ages, hair color, body types, and such. Then he had me study all of the cards to see if I could find the right ones for each of them. It took me a while to go through hundreds of cards, and I could tell Della was getting fidgety. She got up to make more tea. After that, she went downstairs to the bakery Nigel lived above (the aroma of butter and cinnamon wafted up and made my mouth water just sitting there). She brought back pastries called Mill Furry, or something like that. Della said it was French. She handed me one, and it was so flakey and buttery, it literally shattered when I took a bite. I got some on the cards, but Nigel just waved me off when I apologized.

"It'll wipe off. That's why they made them on acetate, I'm sure. Just keep looking, son. When you've finished, I'll get to work."

And he did. Oncet I'd found the right chins and eyes and everything else for those three, he took them and made some sketches using wax pencils. (I finished my Mill Furry while he worked.) He filled in the gaps and showed me. It made my heart ache to see Clarice looking just like herself, pretty and all, smiling at me. I chose a smile for her because she did that a good bit when we were together. The other two pictures—Mama Mae and Clayne—were not as good. Probably because I didn't know them as well and hated them so much. For one thing, Clayne seemed too young. He was only about twenty-four, but he was one of those guys who looked older. More like thirty. And Mama Mae looked too good. When I knew her, she had dark bags under her eyes and her face was drawn—even though she looked sorta overweight. I told Nigel all that along with a few more suggestions, and damned if he didn't get them looking more and more like themselves by the second and third tries.

"Just give me a minute or two more, dear," he said to Della, who was jiggling her keys.

"I'm sorry, Nigel, it's just that traffic is a bear this time of day, and I need to get back and meet up with Alex. We've got a lot of work yet to do."

"I can imagine. You know, I gave up my car, in part, because of the traffic snarls and all the damned great juggernauts hogging the highways. I just take taxis or the Metro," he said without taking his eyes from his work. He erased Clayne's eyebrows, then added a few more details.

"Wow! That's them! That looks just like them! That's going to help us track 'em down."

Della looked kinda worried when I said that and added, "That's one of the things we need to talk about tonight, Abit." Nigel looked at her and nodded. It felt odd—like they were talking to each other as though I weren't in the room.

Whatever, I was just happy we had such good likenesses to work with.

As we were leaving, heading down his stairway, Nigel asked us to hold up a minute. He went back inside and came back out with that painting Della loved so much. He handed it to her and whispered something in her ear. She tried to resist, but I could tell she really wanted it. "Something to remember me by, down in Laurel Falls," he said so I could hear, too.

I saw how tore up she was. She couldn't speak; all she could do was clutch the painting to her heart.

He watched us go down his stairway and when we reached the landing, I turned and said, "Thanks again, Nigel," waving the three pictures. "And come see us."

"I just might, V.J., I just might," I heard him offer as he closed the door. Della didn't say a word as we walked to the car, but she started crying as soon as we got in and closed the doors. She was all busted up over his kindness, so I had to drive. Thank heavens it wasn't far 'cause that D.C. traffic gave me the willies. On the way home, she kept saying that old friends were just the best, irreplaceable. I hoped she meant me, too.

Chapter 10

When we got back to Alex's, I hurried to my room with the pictures of the three Ledbetters and added them to my notes. While I was organizing everything, I looked up and saw Alex standing in the doorway. He seemed more serious than usual, though when I showed him the pictures Nigel'd made, he shared my excitement. Then he just turned and went downstairs.

When I joined them in the kitchen, they were standing round, drinking wine and not saying much, real stiff-like. Della asked me if I wanted something; I helped myself to a beer.

Alex stood over the stove, stirring his spaghetti sauce and adding the meatballs. I finished up the salad I'd made before we went to Nigel's. It included some purslane and chickweed I'd found in Glover Park, where I'd walked Jake. I mentioned that it was from an area too high for dog pee. That got approving nods, but no laughs.

We didn't say much during dinner, but I figured that was because it tasted so good (even better than it smelled), and we were all just shoveling it in. When we'd finished, and I'd cleared the table, Alex started talking about how he and Della had done a lot of research for me on his computer and on the telephone. He used that LexisNexis thing again, like he did when we were working on Lucy's case. It sure paid off then, and I hoped it would again.

Della started explaining how they'd been looking into stories about grifters in the South and finding people to call. I'd already been privy to what good reporters they were and how they could work the phones to get results. In fact, I'd been sleeping better since we got here because of that. But then she stopped, even though they knew I was dying for one of them to go on. When they didn't, I asked, "What else have you found out?"

"Well, we just wanted to make sure you were still interested, because this isn't going to be easy," Alex said.

"Interested? Of course I'm interested. Count me in." I wasn't sure what was going on, but something felt wrong.

"We've found some people you'll want to talk to," Della said, her voice sounding different. Like one of my teachers explaining stuff, instead of my best friend "Several of them were fleeced by a threesome that could be yours. Of course, we can't be sure—they likely changed their names—but when I described them, they all got hopping mad and wanted to know how to get ahold of them. These stories mostly came from all over Virginia, which, when you figure in their visit to your school in North Carolina, tells us they moved around a lot. To stay ahead of the law—if, that is, they were even looking. Lots of folks we talked to couldn't get any traction with their local law enforcement. Some had their stories featured in newspapers—but those just served as warnings to others. They didn't help find the crooks."

"They all seem to have interesting tales to tell," Alex added, "and when you talk to them, they could lead you to more folks. You just never know where this kind of search will take you." He paused while he looked for something and, after rifling through a stack of stuff a foot deep, came out with a stapled pack of papers. "This includes information about con artists I pulled together for you. I'm not sure how it helps—like closing the barn door after the horse got out—but I think you'll take some comfort in how good these cons are at their craft. You need to know what you're talking about when you meet their victims and while you're looking for them."

"Great," I said. "When do we get started?"

"What you mean 'we,' white man?"

I looked at him like he'd lost his marbles.

"You know, the old Lone Ranger and Tonto joke," he said, with a forced smile. When I didn't say anything he added, "Oh, come on. With all the television you've watched—you've seen reruns of that old show, haven't you?"

"Yeah, I've seen the show, but I still don't get it."

"Well, the Lone Ranger says something like, 'This looks bad; we're in a lot of trouble here.' And Tonto says …"

"Oh, I know the joke," I said chuckling, "but what does that have to do with us?"

"You said when are *we* going to search for these con artists."

"Yeah, so?"

"*We* aren't going to search for them. *You* are. Della and I have spent days doing the research for you. Now it's your turn to go talk to these people and find out what you can, on your own." He stopped and said, "I need some coffee. Anyone else?" Della and I nodded.

He left us sitting there, both of us staring straight ahead, not looking at one another. The sounds from the coffee grinder mixed with something that felt like angry waspers buzzing in my head. I got really pissed off that he was fussing with his damn coffee at a time like this. And I couldn't imagine why I said I wanted any. My stomach was in a knot, and I didn't need anything else keeping me awake all night.

Finally, when he came back in, sipping his coffee like we were having a great time at one of his hoity-toity cafés, I blurted out, "You're not going to help me, are you?"

"We *have* helped you, Abit, and we *are* helping you," Alex said. "And we're just a phone call away."

"I'll be waiting for you to call me every evening," Della added.

"But no one will talk to me."

"We will, honey. I'll take your calls, anytime," Della said, patting my arm.

I jerked my arm back. "I don't mean you. I mean them folks. They won't talk to the likes of me."

"Why not?" Alex asked. At that moment, I hated him, standing there with his arms crossed, like a big shot in his fancy home.

"Would you? If you didn't know me ahead of time? Would you open your door to me? At the least, they'll think

I'm a Jehovah's Witness; at the worst, they'll worry I'm another con man."

"I would talk to you if I thought you'd help me catch those grifters," he said. "Just show them the pictures Nigel drew and tell them you want to find them, too. You'll be in the door in no time."

I know I looked upset. Truth be told, I was about to cry. Della jumped in just in time. "Wait a minute, Alex. Abit isn't one of your minions you send out on a research jaunt. Let's back up. We've got our reasons, honey. First, we *know* you can do this. Second, we've laid a lot of groundwork for you. Neither one of us can do this with you—we've set aside too many obligations as it is. And third, you need to do this on your own."

"So, you expect me to go traipsing all over tarnation, all on my own? You can't expect me to do that!"

"Why not?" Alex asked again. Man, he wasn't budging an inch.

I stood up so fast, my chair almost tipped over. I was ready to pick it up and throw it through a window. "You know why not. You think you can just buy me some clothes, dress me up, and send me out into the world. This stinks. This totally stinks. I'm stuck up here, where I have no way of getting home. Then you ask me, all calm-like, like those damn counselors at school, why I can't do this or that. Well, I'll tell you. I can't do this because I'm … I'm *Abit*."

"No, you're V.J., even if I still call you Abit," Alex said. "You know, the V.J. who went back to school and who did so well he became a mentor to other students."

"Yeah, but I can't see me taking the bus all round Virginia. It'd take forever, and Mama will worry about where I am."

"I can't either."

"What do you mean?"

"You can have the Merc," Alex said. I think he expected me to get excited like a little puppy over that. He knew how much I'd loved that car when he drove it down to Laurel Falls. He even taught me to drive in it, but I was still pissed off. Besides, I didn't want to drive *any* car, even the Merc, all over Virginia. I wasn't ready for that, and that's what I told him.

"Okay," he said, folding his notes and putting them in his briefcase. "I guess you're not ready to go back to school or to quit being misunderstood. Maybe Adam's Rib in Laurel Falls will let you wash dishes, and you can live with your mother and father. That sounds like a life well lived."

"Well, maybe it does. You're always going on about not making fun of people who can't do better than that. Now you're turning on me."

"Oh, not so fast. I'm not making fun of people who can't do better. Dishwashing is an honorable job, if that's your best shot. But *you* can do more. That's what I'm making fun of. Your lame vision of what you're capable of."

I didn't know what to say to that, and I was afraid if I opened my mouth, I'd start blubbering. Alex musta realized that because he said, a little nicer, "We can finish talking about this tomorrow, if you want."

But I knew I wouldn't sleep a wink if we left things as they were. I started rambling on with all kinds of excuses even I knew were stupid. Alex interrupted. "Abit, don't worry about all that and just listen, would you? I'm *giving* you the Merc."

"What?"

"Just what I said. You *own* the Merc. It's yours."

I couldn't speak, in part, because my brain just couldn't take it all in. The Merc was mine? And after I'd just thought how much I hated him. Man, I didn't know what to think. Even those waspers stopped buzzing.

"What'll *you* drive?"

"I've ordered a new vehicle. Something more economical to run and better for the environment—a Toyota pickup. It won't do a lot for my image here in D.C., but all these trips down your way mean more to me, anyway. So I had the Merc checked out, tuned up, and new tires put on it. All you have to do is take this title certificate that I've already signed over to you. I'll handle the rest of the paperwork for you."

I hugged him for what felt like five minutes. It wasn't till I saw the spot on his dark shirt that I realized I'd been crying. I felt like such a jerk! "Nothing to be ashamed of, Abit. I caught you off guard," Alex said, patting my back. "I know you hated me just now. I used to think that about my dad, too. I hope you'll feel differently in the morning."

Chapter 11

The glowing clock dial stabbed at my eyes. Two o'clock. It took all my willpower not to wake up Alex so I could ask him more questions about what lay ahead. But he was sleeping with Della, and, well, I wasn't about to go in there.

I lay in bed, my whole body buzzing, and I imagined those roads, chocked full of cars like when Della and I drove into town. How the hell was I gonna drive the Merc out of D.C.? I'd barely driven on small mountain roads. Sure, I was behind the wheel on some trips with Alex to Asheville and back. And I knew that car inside and out. He taught me how to change the oil—the Merc dealers really ripped you off, he said—and I knew how to change tires and the like. But driving on the Beltway? No way. Or any of the other briar patch of roads surrounding the District. Wouldn't you know it? Here I'd got a car of my own, but I couldn't drive it home. As if I had any idea where home was anymore.

I turned on my light and started reading the stuff Alex gave me about con artists. I wanted to find out all I could about those bastards. At first, it just covered what Della and Alex had already told me—that cons take advantage of people's needs and habits. That sure struck a chord. I thought back to how they'd listened to what I'd said and read my mind, not like magicians but by studying me. From that, they knew just how to play me.

As I read on, I could see how they'd worked all of us like a textbook case—they got us to feel some sympathy and give just a little money, at first. Then they asked for a little more. And more. When they had us all softened up, they went for the strike with the director, playing to his greed. I had to hand it them—they were impressive, in a nasty kinda way.

I'd heard the expression pig in a poke all my life, and I knew it meant getting ahold of something—or longing for something—without knowing enough about it. That's what the director did, buying land that wasn't for sale. But when I thought about it, most things in life were a pig in a poke. I didn't know Clarice, and I didn't check her out. I trusted my feelings for her, which was exactly what con artists were banking on, so to speak. Besides, on a practical level, no one had time for all that investigating. Who could ever do that— or want to be *that* suspicious of one another? But I could see how ever since that first time I saw Clarice, when she was traipsing through the pasture, the sun lighting up her hair and gauzy dress, I'd made her into something special. And Clayne and his mama musta been sitting back laughing their heads off that I fell for her like that.

After I read more of the file, I felt like one of them hamsters running round in a little wheel. That was what most of us were. We had feelings, cared about people, and for that we got rewarded by being ripped off by people who didn't care about others. Only to have it happen all over again, year after year, regular enough they could write long reports about it. My case was just like all the others. And nobody was doing anything about it, and nobody ever would. Or *could*. Because who didn't feel lonely or unlistened to or unimportant, at least some of the time? Some of us for longer, but still, always fresh meat for them to sink their teeth into.

You'd've thought reading that report woulda gotten me all riled up, and it did at first, but as I read on, it wore me down. So much conniving against good folks depressed me. I put the papers down, turned out the light, and finally got to sleep.

The next morning, I woke up late. By then, Alex and Della were out, so I still couldn't talk to them. I made myself some toast, and I saw they'd left coffee in a thermos for me. (They'd never've let it sit on the burner for too long.) Jake hung round for some scraps (I gave him the burned toast corners), and we went out for a walk.

I felt easier now walking round town, at least that small section of Georgetown, and I was ready to see more of it. I'd studied the map in Alex's office, and the roads looked like a grid—not like the windy roads back in Laurel Falls. Jake and I walked along P Street for blocks and blocks, passing by Stead Park, which was pretty small compared to the parks we were used to, but better than nothing. Jake agreed. Then we passed through Logan Circle, where who else but General Logan sat atop a fine-looking horse. We took a few short detours when Jake spotted some squirrels and eventually crossed over Rock Creek. About then, things started looking familiar, and before I knew it, I was in

Dupont Circle, where Della used to live and write her
stories.

It was a whirlwind of traffic, cars speeding round and
round the circle, people in all states of dress and undress
lying on the grass, while old men and young men and some
black men played chess in a park-like area. Coffee shops
and restaurants lined the streets that came off the circle like
sun rays in a kid's drawing. I felt them waspers again,
reminding me how much I could never drive here.

I wanted to take a closer look at the train station, so I
picked up Jake and tucked him under my arm. We ventured
down a short flight of steps before I nearly fell over from a
case of the dizzies. The longest damned escalator I'd ever
seen (truth be known, the only ones I'd ever seen were on
TV) went so deep I couldn't see the bottom. People were
rushing and bumping, mostly saying "excuse me," and two
stopped to pat Jake. He musta remembered living there,
because he took it more in stride than I did.

We got outta there, and as we headed up the street, I
spotted that bakery below Nigel's apartment. I tied Jake up
(I wasn't too worried someone would steal him) and went
inside. I had a devil of a time figuring out what I wanted.
Maybe, it dawned on me, that was because it was the first
time I'd ever bought my own food! Even at school,
everything was paid for, and there weren't places close by
to skip out to. I took my coffee and some kinda flaky
chocolate roll outside to the table where I'd tied Jake.
Someone was giving him part of a biscuit, so he was happy.

As I ate the fudgy roll, my tongue and mouth went crazy. It was like nothing I'd ever had before. While I was chewing, I couldn't help wondering what I'd be if I'd been born in a different place. Like this one. My life would look nothing like it did, and I'd likely feel better about myself. And I'd've gotten a good education. Not that my life would've been perfect, but I knew that I'd be somebody else, and I liked that idea. I probably wouldn't be afraid of driving those streets, and I'd know how to pronounce that delicious roll I'd just eaten.

That led me to thinking how totally cool it would be to pop up and say hey to Nigel. Like I lived in D.C. and knew someone. As I drank my coffee, though, I knew I'd never get up the nerve to do that.

As it turned out, I didn't need to.

"Well, hello, hello, hello! V.J., what brings you here all alone?"

"Hey, Nigel," I said as I scrambled to stand up to greet him proper-like. "And I'm not alone, I'm with Jake." I tugged on Jake's leash to bring him out from under the table where he was scoffing up crumbs.

"Oh, wonderful! So glad to finally meet Della's faithful companion." He fussed over Jake, scratching him behind his ears and just above his tail. I could tell he knew his way round dogs. "While you're here, dear boy, I have something I want to show you. Won't you pop up for a moment? Though let me grab a little something first."

LYNDA McDANIEL

While Nigel was inside the bakery, I watched through the big window as he waited in line, and I had to chuckle. He had on another suit and tie, only this time no vest, just a plaid shirt with a knit tie. I figured that was his idea of casual. When he came out, he had a coffee and giant cinnamon roll that looked even better than Mrs. Parker's. Man, I'd've been fat as a pig if I lived above a bakery, though the challenge might've been worth it.

I brushed crumbs off my shirt and pants and untied Jake. We headed up the stairs together, and as he opened his door, Nigel made an "after you" gesture.

We sat at his kitchen table, in front of a sunny window looking down on the circle. When he'd finished what he called his elevenses, he brought in a tablet of drawing paper. "I certainly enjoyed that exercise when you and Della were here. I didn't realize I'd have the pleasure of seeing you again, but I'm glad I have. I was just practicing ..." He showed me the pictures of Mama Mae, Clayne, and Clarice, but now they looked even more like themselves—and in full color. "They're not that different from what you already have, but based on some of the details you shared, I fixed a few things and added color." He handed them to me. "Perhaps they will help your search."

"Wow! These are even better than the black-and-whites! And they *will* help me, if I can actually do this."

"How's that?"

"Well, I'm scared to death to drive here. I mean, I *did* drive home the other day, but that's just a few blocks. I'm talking about that tangle of highways and all."

"Nothing to be embarrassed about, V.J. I believe I mentioned that I gave up my car a number of years ago for the same reason. Those blighters! Bloody idiots racing to and fro." Then he got a worried look on his face and added, "Oh, I hope I haven't compounded your concerns. You'll do just fine, like the millions of people who manage it every day. When are you heading out?"

"I'm not sure, but soon. And there's another problem. I just found out last night Della isn't coming with me. They expect me to traipse all over Virginia and talk to strangers all on my own. They just sprung it on me, and I acted like an ass." Not sure why I told him that, but it felt good to talk about it. "To be honest, I'd like to stay right here in town and never go back."

Nigel got a worried look and said, "Don't underestimate how important this trip is for you." I figured he was about to give me the same talk Della and Alex did, and I started to get my back up. I mean, who was this guy to tell me what to do? He didn't even know me like Della did. "I'm not just talking about going back to school, or even catching these scoundrels, V.J. This trip is even more important than that. As you go deeper into your travels, I believe you'll discover more than you can imagine."

That caught me off guard and made me feel uneasy, though I wasn't sure why. I had no idea what he was talking about, but it felt like that time at the circus when a creepy mechanical fortune teller pushed a card toward me that read, "Use great caution to avoid losing something of value." I couldn't ever quite shake off that warning. It'd hovered over me ever since, popping up now and again to cast a dark shadow over good times.

Nigel and I chatted a little longer, moving into more familiar territory like how Della was doing with the store and how Jake liked Laurel Falls. But in the back of my mind, I was still thinking about what he'd just said about my trip.

When I stood to leave, I gave him a hug at the door, which seemed to startle him. If I was going on this trip, I needed to remember that not everyone was used to so much hugging. I don't know where or why I came by that—it sure didn't happen much in our house when I was growing up. Then again, maybe that was why.

Nigel handed me a card as I was about to head down the steps. I nearabout dropped it, Jake tugging at me to go. "You can call me anytime, V.J. I'd like to hear how things are going, and if I can help in any way ..."

At first, I didn't know what to make of it—his business card. Had anyone ever given me one before? No, not even Alex. I studied it for a moment and thanked him. "Who knows, Nigel," I said on the way down the stairs, "maybe I *will* call you from Timbuktu!"

Chapter 12

As Jake and I turned into Alex's driveway, my stomach lurched. I'd hoped they were still gone, since I was dreading facing them after last night. But there sat Della's Jeep and the Merc. And a new truck parked on the street in front of the house. Never before had I seen a shiny pickup in front of anywhere I'd lived.

When I went inside, I heard Della upstairs on the phone in Alex's office; Alex was working on the back porch. I went up and knocked on the office door, even though the door was open. Della held her finger up, like people do when they want you to wait a minute. Jake didn't know about such a gesture and went flying in, trying to get in her lap. She told the caller she had to go.

"Hello, Jakey Boy. Did you miss me?" They smooched and hugged. Then Della broke the ice. "You feeling any better today?"

"Yeah, I'm getting used to the idea. I'm sorry about …"

"No need for that, honey. We really threw you a curve. Let's just let it go. Are you hungry?"

We both worked on the BLTs, and Jake weaseled some bacon out of each of us. When Alex joined us, we sat down to lunch.

"I just got off the phone with Jewel Johnston in Staunton," Della said oncet we'd finished. "We don't know anything for sure, but I found this newspaper story about her." She passed me a printed copy of the article. "She was ripped off for about $3,000, which was her life savings. The article said it was just one man, but that he mentioned his mother to Jewel. It sounds as though they fit your folks, Abit. And with Nigel's artwork, you should be able to get an ID right away."

"Did the cops try to find them?" I asked as I reached for a couple of the chocolate chip cookies she'd made (though I couldn't figure out when).

"I don't think they tried very hard," Della said. "Ms. Johnston reported them, but lots of victims won't go to the police—like your lily-livered director at the school. He screwed you over rather than coming clean with the cops and helping find those bastards." Della's face was getting red, but I'd seen her get like that before—when somebody did something to hurt people she cared for.

"Old man Henson was always a pain in the ass, making up rules just to make himself feel important," I said. "Thing was, he *was* important. He had a good job at a great school. What was his problem?"

"Abit, I'm sure I don't need to tell you that people are idiots a lot of the time," Alex said. "Even decent folks." I musta made a face, because he added, "I'm not saying Henson is a great guy. At the very least, he made a bad mistake, and he's a chicken shit to lay it on a twenty-year-old boy."

"Man," I corrected.

"Soon."

"What do you mean?" I asked.

"We're heading out tomorrow."

"Why so fast? We just got here? I could help you find more people. Just show me how to work that machine ..."

Della put her hand on my arm, trying to console me. "It's been four days, honey, and I've got to get back to the store. Billie called and said there's something weird going on down there. I've got to go back, so we need to leave right after rush hour tomorrow morning."

"What's going on at the store?"

"I don't know yet—I'll let you know when you call me in the evenings." She gave me four rolls of quarters and told me not to spend them on chips and candy, like I was a kid. "You can call me or Alex anytime you need. And what about your mother? Do you need to check in so she knows you're all right?"

"Nah, she hates talking on the phone. When I'm at school, I write her oncet a week—just a postcard or something short."

"Okay, but don't buy a postcard from some scenic overlook in Virginia." She was laughing, so I knew she didn't think I was that stupid.

Normally, I'd feel like a baby having to check in every night, but I was glad she'd be there for me. I felt better for about a minute until those words "rush hour" sank in. Alex did that thing again.

"Della will drive her Jeep, and I'll take you in the Merc as far as Strasburg. She'll wait for me, and then you're on your own."

How will you get back to D.C.?" I asked.

"Don't worry about it," he said. "We've got that all worked out. I just want to help get you get started."

And that's how I got outta that crazy D.C. traffic. As things turned out, traffic was the least of my troubles.

Chapter 13

Della and her lead foot were long gone by the time Alex and I drove away from his house in the Merc. When he pulled over at a gas station in Strasburg, she was already there, standing by the Jeep, sipping a coffee. Alex filled up the Merc's tank and gave me the keys. Then he added, "Don't spend this all in one place" and handed me a new wallet filled with more twenty dollar bills than I'd ever seen at one time. He seemed kinda sad, maybe even a little worried. I shared those feelings, with a giant jolt of fear thrown in. I just mumbled my thanks and gave him a hug. I was taller than him now, which felt good. Like I'd growed up some. I hoped enough.

I'd already had a big goodbye with Della and Jake, so I slipped in behind the steering wheel. "And don't forget to call Della tonight," was the last thing I heard Alex say as I pulled the door shut. He and Della waved their hands out their windows as they sped past me, and I could see Jake looking out the back window till they disappeared over a hill.

It wasn't till my hands began to ache that I realized how hard I'd been gripping the steering wheel. My knuckles were white as holly wood. And I hadn't even cranked the car yet! Finally, I started the Merc and pulled out onto

Highway 11. When a few folks honked at me, I noticed the speedometer said I was going only twenty mile an hour in a fifty-five zone. But oncet I got about ten mile down the road, I was up to fifty.

I'd done some solo driving before, including a big old Ford truck at the school. That damn truck had the lousiest gear box—it slipped outta third and locked in second in the blink of an eye. I figured out how to shift real easy-like most of the time, but when it locked, I got myself outta some jams by lifting the hood and manually putting that truck into the right gear. So I knew my way round car trouble.

I'd heard Alex and Della say their minds did some fanciful thinking while driving on long car trips. I'd experienced a little of that on the way up with Della, but I wasn't driving. I figured as the driver, I'd need to concentrate on the center line and all the other things to keep the car safely in its lane. But near a place called Hillsburg, I had a sense of the road, and I started to relax. My mind drifted off to explore the notion that right then I could drive *anywhere* I wanted. I had a full tank of gas, money in my pocket, and for the first time in my life, I was free. I pictured myself turning right and crossing the country, heading toward California, paying my way by working odd jobs and sleeping in the Merc. But someone started honking at me again (I'd slowed down too much while daydreaming), so I sped up and kept the wheels headed south.

When I checked my rearview mirror to see what his problem was, I noticed Della had added something to the car, dangling from the mirror. I guessed I hadn't seen it at first—I musta thought it was one of those pine-tree air fresheners everyone had back home—but up close I saw it was a picture of the school she'd cut out and hung with a rubber band. My heart did that funny thing—like a bellows opening and closing—when I saw that beautiful campus. That picture gave me added courage.

On the passenger seat, I'd laid out the map Alex had made that showed me how I could avoid the interstates. I'd have to do a little backtracking because there were folks he thought I should see sooner rather than later. Like the woman I was headed toward—Jewel Johnston, the one who'd lost her home and savings in Staunton. That town, Alex told me last night, was pronounced *STAN-ton*, which made no sense whatsoever. As if life weren't hard enough, people went and did stupid things like changing the way letters were pronounced.

Della'd packed me a cooler with everything inside fitting neatly together, like a jigsaw puzzle. A stack of sandwiches was wrapped in wax paper atop an icepack to keep me from getting sick (Like Mama, she was always worried about food going bad. I figured that store had beat that into her. She had enough troubles without folks claiming her food poisoned them!)

Next to the sandwiches (ham/swiss and roast chicken), she'd added apples and oranges, gingerbread cookies she'd bought at Nigel's bakery and the chocolate chip ones she'd made, a bag of mixed nuts, beef jerky, and a thermos of coffee. It all looked so pretty I didn't want to wreck it—a notion that lasted about one more mile. I pulled over just outside Staunton and found a town park with a picnic table.

Some kids were climbing all over the playground, and I spotted a man and woman watching them. When one of the boys fell off the jungle gym, the mother stood to go help him. I heard the father say, "Leave him. You'll make a sissy of him." But the kid was screaming. Maybe hurt. She jerked her arm out of her husband's grasp and went to her boy. I could almost feel how good her hug felt.

Something about that scene made me go funny inside. It seemed kinda familiar, and then I realized how at that moment, I felt as scared as that kid. My stomach tightened with dread at what lay ahead. How was I ever gonna do all this on my own?

But then that little boy just jumped up and started playing like he was happy again. His mama had made him feel like he could go back to the terrors of the jungle gym. That reminded me of Andy and Jasper—those two young'uns I mentored at school. I recalled how they'd cried when I left, but I didn't give them any comfort like that mama just did. I was too messed up myself. I did hug them, but I told them I didn't know when I'd be back, which made them cry more. I realized that even though I didn't want to be on this trip, if I ever wanted to see them two again, I didn't have much choice.

As I started in on one of the roast chicken sandwiches, a little chickadee sweetened the afternoon with a series of chick-a-dee-dee-dees. He moved closer, and I swear he was staring at me, whistling for some of my bread. I threw a tiny

THE ROADS TO DAMASCUS

piece in his direction, and he pecked it into smaller pieces and ate them. I saved another crust for him, but I drew the line with the cookies. After I ate two of them and drank some coffee, I started studying Alex's map and found the address for Ms. Johnston. I felt a kinship with her and her troubles, but I was still struggling with the idea of going up to a strange woman's house and asking her to let me in so we could talk. Never mind that I wanted to talk about con artists. I figured she'd slam the door in my face.

I cranked the Merc and twisted round town for a while, making some wrong turns. On the highway, I hadn't noticed so much what Della hated about the Merc—the way it rattled and turned people's heads—but on these small roads, I saw how folks looked up as I drove by.

I passed some old Victorian homes that looked pretty nice, but the address I needed wasn't downtown. It was quite a ways out. I finally found Ms. Johnston's neighborhood and parked in a dirt patch in front of her address. I sat there a while, getting up my nerve. I looked at that picture of the school hanging from the mirror and gave myself a pep talk. I could hear Della's voice in my head, and that went a long ways toward getting my fingers on the door handle.

I stepped out of the car and brushed the crumbs off my pants. I sure was glad Alex had gotten me some new clothes. At least I looked presentable. Back at school, we dressed pretty much for comfort, which had gotten more and more sloppy until the school had to put its foot down about pajama pants. (Though they were hard to tell from the loose pants all the hippies wore.)

I walked up the path to her trailer. It had seen better days, the only decoration on the drab beige siding was the rust crawling down from the roof and round all the doors and windows, leaving a trail of reddish-brown streaks. But even this late in the season, the front yard was still a riot of color, a well-tended garden trying its best to produce one more tomato and marigold before a killing frost.

I knocked, and a woman came to the door, clutching her bathrobe—at one o'clock in the afternoon. When she had a coughing fit, I realized she had a bad cold. "Yes?" her voice croaked through the glass storm door, before she launched into another fit.

I sure didn't want to catch her cold, but I'd come this far, and I needed to talk with her. Except I couldn't. I was nearabout frozen with fear, and the words just stuck in my throat. "I, er, wondered if I might talk, er ..." I gave up, pulled out Nigel's drawings of the three of them con artists, and blurted, "Do you know these folks?"

She unclutched her bathrobe, and it fell open, showing an old flannel nightie like Mama wore. "Who are you?" she asked. "Why are you botherin' me with this crap now? No one's done anything in two years. I lost my home, and I'm living in this shithole." She clutched her robe again and started to cry.

The damnedest thing: I started to cry, too. I couldn't help myself, because to be honest, I wasn't just crying for her but for me, too. It was like I was finally able to let it out.

When my tears turned into the waterworks, she opened her door, and said, "Oh, honey. Did they fuck you, too?"

Chapter 14

Ms. Johnston introduced herself and insisted I call her Jewel. She motioned for me to sit on her sofa while she put the kettle on. And some clothes. The trailer was spotless inside, and she'd made it as nice as she could with photos and houseplants and some pottery pieces. I could tell she'd put a fresh slipcover on the old sofa and chairs because a coupla year ago, I helped Mama do the same.

When she came back, she sat opposite me in a big overstuffed chair. That's when I got a good look at her. While she was away, she'd run a comb through her hair and put on some lipstick, because she looked kinda pretty, in spite of her cold and all. She tried to put a good face on, but I could see the sorrow in her eyes. Like the fire had gone out.

Even so, something about them (the bluest I'd ever seen) drew me in. I leaned right into them, as I sat on the edge of the sofa, hanging on her every word.

"I'm embarrassed by how I look," she said, running her fingers through her hair. "I got this damn cold last week, and I can't shake it."

"Well, I just barged in on you, so please don't give it a thought. You've got a nice place here, and it feels like I'm back home with Mama." She winced when I said that, but I knew she had to be pushing sixty because of Alex's research and the mortgage papers he found. She probably didn't want to be reminded of her age, so I let that conversation die.

Eventually, we began sharing our war stories over a really good cup of tea. I tasted the lemon and honey, which seemed to help her cough. After a few sips, she said she wished she had something more to offer me to go with the tea.

"Hold on a minute," I said and jumped up and ran out the door. I went to the car and rummaged round, coming back in with my stash of chocolate chip and gingerbread cookies. Her face lit up, taking a world of hurt from her eyes, for a moment, anyways. She reached for a chocolate chip cookie.

"Oh, I haven't had a homemade cookie in a year or more. What with my finances, and now I've got the sugar. But I'm having one. I'll just be careful the rest of the day."

We munched for a while before she started her story. Seems Clayne, though he told her his name was Bobby Joe, came to her house selling reverse mortgages. That whole idea was kinda new to her, so she told him she wanted to find out more. She went to her bank, and they told her yep, those mortgages were legit. In fact, they could help her with one. She told me she was kicking herself for not taking *them* up on it, but Bobby Joe had been so nice to her. "I felt some fool loyalty to that young man who introduced me to the idea. Can you believe that?" she asked.

She looked like she was about to cry again, so I added real quick-like, "Oh, I *can* believe it. I've done stuff like that my whole life. My friend Della tells me to be more careful. That I—you, too, I can already tell—have a good heart, and people can take advantage of that. And if it makes you feel any better, about thirty people back home fell for their story. I said 'their' because, at least in North Carolina, his mother works these cons with him."

"Yes, I met her when I was signing the papers and giving him my money." She dabbed at her eyes, maybe from her cold, but likely not. "I lost my home because of them," she said, looking round the old trailer she had to live in. Then she reached over to the table next to her chair and picked up some fabric and needle and thread and began sewing what looked a quilt top. Her hands worked nimbly, and I could tell she'd made plenty of quilts before.

Back home, I'd always felt sad the way women worked so hard making a Bear's Paw or Blazing Star quilt from knit scraps they'd get free from the T-shirt factory. All that hard work, and it ended up looking like a big pair of droopy drawers. But Jewel's Flower Garden (I was pretty sure that was the pattern) was different. The fabric scraps were fresh and colorful. She caught me looking at her hands.

"They stole my home and a good bit of my pride, but they cain't take this from me," she said, nodding at her quilt. "I've made all kinds of patterns; I don't even know how many, but I can still make something pretty from little scraps and whatever I find along the way." We sat quiet-like, honoring what she'd just said. Then we started in on them two again.

"The thing that makes them so good—and bad—is they don't ask for a lot of money. I know there's that expression, 'Don't steal anything small,' but it seemed to work for them. I trusted them because they asked for a reasonable application fee. But then they added on insurance and other fees my bank manager later explained were 'predatory cross-marketing.'"

"What does that mean? The one about stealing small?"

"Oh, just that you'd pay the price for stealing something small as much as something big, so why not go big? But the penalty is bigger, and people's suspicions are stronger."

I could tell Jewel felt bad reliving all that, but her story made me feel better. It showed that they worked in a way that could fool you—so you trusted them. I started telling her some of what I'd read up on about con artists, like the way they faked being like you and preyed on the compassion you showed them.

"Oh, yeah, you've got that right," Jewel said. "And his mother—I believe she went by Mildred—talked to me about the peace of mind she'd gained since she had this kind of mortgage." Jewel's face got real red, and she fell into a terrible coughing fit. I figured I'd better cut this session short. I didn't want her to get sicker with me stirring it all up again. Besides, I was fuming about that battleax using Mama's name for no good.

"I don't know how you carry on so good," I said. "You don't seem bitter."

"Well, I may live in a dump, but there's good in my life, too. A couple of years ago I learned to go to bed each night and think about what I was grateful for. I've never been all that good at praying—it always felt like a vending-machine religion to keep asking for more, even for others—

but I took to this and do it most nights. It can be a struggle sometimes, but you'd be amazed at what we have to be thankful for."

I didn't know what to say to that. I knew right off I was grateful for Della and Alex, Jake and the Merc, but before they showed up in my life, well, I would've been stumped. We sat for a moment more before I started packing up my stuff. That was when Jewel said, "You seem like a nice boy."

I didn't know how to respond to that. I always felt embarrassed whenever someone complimented me. She looked closer at me and added, "Oh, did that take that from you, too?"

"What?"

"Your Self. Your pride."

"Nah, I don't reckon I had that to steal."

She walked me to her door and out into the front garden. By then, I felt as comfortable round Jewel as, say, Mary Lou, Duane's wife. And she musta liked me, too, because she told me if I were ever in the area again to please stop by. Of course, I knew back home that was just what folks said to get rid of you.

I tried to leave her the tin of cookies, but she reminded me she had the sugar. (I'd've been lying if I didn't admit I was relieved.) As we walked down her path to the road, I stopped. "Say, do you know why people call this town STAN-ton when it ain't spelled that way?"

Jewel laughed for the first time since I'd met her. "They say some mayor long ago didn't want his town pronounced like a Brit would, but who knows? Who cares?" That about summed it up.

She kept walking with me as I headed to my car. Said she needed to get a bit of fresh air, but it was like we were both sad to say goodbye. She was smiling and waving when I started the Merc, but her face changed in an instant. She looked worried and made the gesture to roll down my window.

"Honey, you be careful with that car. It's pretty distinct, and I know these folks. Or their kind, anyways. You stir things up too much, and they'll come a-looking for you."

Chapter 15

"He's at a funeral. For his cousin, I believe."

The woman standing in the doorway looked a lot like Cleva—big boned, big bosomed, and if she behaved like Cleva, big hearted. She'd let her long hair go silver, like Cleva's, but unlike Cleva's (which was always in a bun), hers hung loose and flipped at the ends, like two waterfalls coming outta the top of her head. She had on a big white apron that looked like it'd overseen more than a few pies and meatloaves.

I'd driven down Hwy. 252 to Middlebrook, circling back round to just south of Staunton, to meet the next person on Alex's list. (Alex had warned me this trip wouldn't be on a straight path, and he wasn't kidding.) I hoped this one paid off better than the dead ends I spoke to after Jewel. Either they'd been conned by someone a lot older than the Ledbetters, or they knew the person who did it—just couldn't do much about it. And one guy hadn't been ripped off at all; he looked at me like I was crazy and told me to get lost. But it wasn't a total loss. As I drove round for a couple of days and talked to those folks, I started feeling better about being on my own. In fact, I was liking the newness of everything.

Burlon McMillan, the guy at the funeral, could be kin to the Ledbetters, according to Alex's research. I'd asked Alex if that was a good idea—I mean their being kin, and all. I had to laugh when he reminded me that half your kin likes you, and the other half would help lock you up, so the odds were fifty- fifty. Okay, but I still needed to figure out how to approach him since I didn't think a family funeral was a good time to ask him if he was related to a bunch of crooks.

"Any idea when he'll be back?

"Well, if that funeral is like others around here, they'll be drinking and carrying on afterwards," she said, frowning. Maybe she was more like Mama than Cleva. "You're welcome to wait here, uh, what's your name?"

"V.J. Bradshaw."

"What kind of name is Veejay?"

"You can call me Abit."

"Okay, Abbott. You can wait in the kitchen. I could use the company—Mr. McMillan ain't never home, and I get bored and lonesome with all the chores I have to do for him. Besides, you look like you could use a piece or two of fried chicken."

Like I said, I was feeling better about this trip. As I walked into the entryway, she shook my hand and told me her name was Nadine. Then she opened the kitchen door and let out the smell of wood smoke mixed with bacon and apple pie. She set me up on a barstool at the kitchen counter, pulled her hair back in a bun by twisting it just so, and started pulling things out of the fridge—a roast chicken, a bowl of something covered with tinfoil, and some kind of pie with a top crust perfectly browned and shining with a thin layer of melted sugar. Oncet she laid out the spread, she went over to the sink and tackled a pile of dishes. While I ate, I watched her working hard at chores that would never end, and I felt a pang for her and Mama and anyone else who worked in their homes without enough thank-yous to make it all worthwhile.

After I polished off two drumsticks, a mound of bean salad, and a big slice of apple pie, I decided to show her Nigel's drawings. My heart sank when she didn't recognize them, but then I learned she was only Burlon's housekeeper. "His wife's been gone about four year," she told me, "and I'm the fifth housekeeper he's had." She looked over her shoulder and kinda whispered, "He's a right bastard."

She finished the dishes and began making something over at what Mama calls her Hoosier cupboard—a dandy piece of furniture that has a built-in flour bin and sifter, plus a pull-out countertop for more room to work. Below that, there was a large cabinet with shelves for storing baking dishes and such. When I was a kid, I liked to watch Mama use the sifter. She'd just stick her bowl under there and turn the crank, flour magically coming down like snow. One time, I set up some of my toy soldiers under there and pretended they were caught in a snowstorm. (Like I said, *one* time.) I didn't know whether to tell Nadine what the Ledbetters had been up to or not. I decided to say we had some money matters to take care of.

"Well, that don't surprise me. He's tight as a witch's tit, or whatever that expression is. Half the time I have to wait till he's drunk to rifle through his wallet to get paid." She lifted a rolling pin as she said that (she was making another pie), and I figured she could take care of herself, even if Burlon was as bad as she made out.

And he was.

We heard the front door open and slam shut. A tall man looking like Waylon Jennings came stomping into the kitchen, dressed all in black, which, of course, was fitting for a funeral. (Though I got the impression this was his usual wardrobe.) I hoped like the devil it weren't Burlon, but no such luck. Deep shadows blooming beneath his dark eyes and a three-day beard gave him a menacing look. And he was stinkin' drunk. I wiped my mouth with my napkin and eased off the stool. He looked up at me surprised-like.

"Who the hell are *you*?"

I felt heat come offa him as he glared at me, intensifying his smell of drink and sorrow. I felt both repulsed by him and sad for him. "I'm sorry for your loss, sir," I said. I felt kinda stupid quoting a TV show, but I honestly didn't know what else to say.

"Well, la-di-dah. Who are you to come in here sounding like Magnum, P.I.?"

Oh man, he had my number. I just stood there, unable to think of anything else to say. I was halfway wishing he'd just go ahead and throw me out so I could head down the highway and find someone sober to talk to. My other half figured I'd better stick with it. I pulled out the pictures of his kinfolk, even though my gut was telling me it weren't the right time.

"Where the hell you get pictures like that, sonny? They look all sweet and nice, like you get at the mall, come Christmas or Easter."

Really? I thought to myself. But then I hated these folks, which I knew colored my thinking. Maybe he liked them. Or worked with them. He hadn't answered my question, but he did make me curious why this picture reminded him of special times.

"I knew these folks, and I liked them a lot," I said. That was true, for a while, at least for Mama Mae and Clarice. "Then they just up and left, and I want to find them again."

"You say they was nice to you?" he asked. "Then I know you're a-lying. Them two have never been nice to no one. They stole some money and camping equipment of mine before they headed out this last time. Where you from?"

"North Carolina."

"Where?"

"Laurel Falls."

"Never heard of it. But that's the way they travel. Well, I'm sorry they besmirched our family name oncet again." He paused and rubbed his forehead, like the drink was starting to make it hurt. "But I don't know you from Adam, and I'm in no mood today to have you coming round maligning my family when I've just put one in the ground."

"Who says I want to malign them?" I didn't exactly know what that word meant, but it couldn't be something good, considering how much spit he put behind it.

"Why else would you be coming round, showing that damn picture like the FBI?" He sat down and started eating from the pie pan. Nadine frowned but turned back to her new pie. "Listen, I'm no fool. I know that nobody just wants to find them three," he said, kinda giving in. "That woman and her son are bigger screwups than I am, and that little slut Clayne married? She'd sleep with everyone in the county, and I mean *everyone*. He couldn't've put an ad in the paper for 'Bitch Wanted' and found a bigger one."

I had to look away. At Nadine. Out the window. At my feet. Anywhere to hide my face as I wrestled with the notion that I'd been kissing a *married* woman. Clarice had told me they were sister and brother. I wondered why Clayne favored his Mama, but Clarice looked so different. Then a lightbulb came on, and it all made sense, in a way. If Clarice was miserable in her marriage, and they were making her do things she didn't want to do, naturally she'd turn to someone else to care about her.

"Oh, cat's got your tongue? Or was it that bitch who had your tongue and goodness knows what else?"

I could feel my face get hot, and Nadine musta took pity on me, 'cause she told him to get out of her kitchen; she had work to do. I could almost hear the argument going on his head, like it was *his* kitchen, but he was paying her to work in it. Money won, of course, and he headed toward the back of the house. But before he left, he shouted at me, "Get out of my house. Bad family is still family, and who are you to come round here trying to find them and lock them up?"

Nadine got her broom awful close to his feet, and he high-stepped it toward the door.

I couldn't let that go. This may have been only my fourth day on their trail, but it was my twelfth day of having them weigh heavy on me. "You mean ole bastard," I said to his back. "Who are you to blindly defend outlaws who've done damage to so many? And who you seem to know should be locked up. You oughta be ashamed of yourself. They've ruint my life, and I'm gonna find them—for me and all the others they've hurt. And the ones they won't be able to hurt in the future." My heart hammered so hard I was sure he and Nadine could hear it.

Burlon turned back, his eyes a-blazing. He started to say something, but then it was like the fire just went out of him. He shuffled off when Nadine shooed him again with her broom, but not without slamming the kitchen door as he went.

"I think you'd better run along, Abbott," Nadine said, softly. She handed me some biscuits with ham inside, wrapped in wax paper. "I wished I knew something to help. Burlon's got a cousin out the road there about thirty mile, so maybe he can tell you something." She scribbled a name and address on the back of a brown sack, took back the biscuits, and put them inside. As she handed me the bag, she added, "Good luck, boy. I like your spunk!"

Chapter 16

"I hate this godawful trip!" I shouted to no one but me, as I wound my way south. Up ahead, I saw a road sign that read "Rough Road Ahead." "No shit!" I shouted again.

Not long after leaving Burlon's, I stopped the car in a small town so I could walk off my nerves. I couldn't believe how nasty that man was, and I could tell it weren't just the whiskey talking. When I got back to the car, I felt so spent I laid down in the backseat. I couldn't exactly sleep, but I musta dozed some because next thing I knew the sun was coming in low through the back window.

I cranked the Merc and drove a ways, stopping at a jot-em-down store for some Dr. Pepper, water, and whatnot. I got back in the car and pulled out Nadine's ham biscuits. Man, that woman could bake! When I finished, I poured the rest of the thermos coffee I'd gotten at my breakfast diner and ate the last of the apples and cookies (mostly broken now) Della'd packed. That reminded me to call Della, and I headed over to the payphone out front of the store and dialed her at home. We'd already talked a few times since I'd left D.C., so when she picked up, I just said, "I quit!"

"No hello, no how are you?"

"Sorry, but I've had a time of it today. As bad as it was to sit crying with Jewel, I just got cussed out by a man as mean as a rattlesnake. I don't know about this idea of yours." She didn't say anything, which was worse than a lecture. Finally, I broke the standoff. "Okay, okay. You made your point. But it still sucks."

"Tell me what's going on, Abit. Why do you already feel like giving up?"

"I'm not giving up. I'm quitting a lame-brained idea. There's a difference." I could hear her kinda chuckle. She liked it when I stood up for myself. "I don't know why you're laughing. You haven't been driving all over tarnation and getting your ass chewed."

"I did my share of driving today, too, and I *have* had my ass chewed."

"What's going on down there?"

"Later. First, I want to hear what you've been up to. Oh, wait, before I forget, Elbert asked about you. I told him you *weren't* here to stay! But then I told him you'd be back soon."

Elbert Totherow was our favorite beekeeper who was always making excuses about his front porch being chocked full of junk. Every time we drove up, he'd step out to greet us and tell us they weren't moving, they were there to stay. Hearing his greeting by way of Della just made me feel more homesick.

I brought her up to date, and by the time I finished, I didn't feel so bad. Della's a great listener, probably one of the reasons she was such a good reporter. Then she said all the right things, and I calmed down more. By then, I was ready to get the spotlight offa me. "Okay, what's your story?" I asked.

"Oh, there's a real brouhaha going on down here."

I didn't know what a brouhaha was, but I figured it was a mess, based on what she shared next. Seemed some women had gone on strike inside Coburn's, her store back home in Laurel Falls. Its full name was Coburn's General Store, though none of us could remember who Coburn was—even the old-timers. There was no point in renaming it, neither, 'cause no one would've used the new name. It was just Coburn's. Anyways, Della told me some women were tired of their husbands "lording over them," as they put it. So for three days, they'd been showing up every morning and staying till closing time.

"Is Mama one of them?" I asked.

"No, honey, she's not. But she's shown some support. She baked the women your favorite apple cake and brought it over one day when Vester had gone off for supplies."

"What're they so mad about?"

"They're not really mad. I think they're, well as you'd say, give out. Like when their husbands come in and make them take things out of their baskets and put them back on the shelves. And lots of these men are retired, but the women aren't. They still have to do all the cleaning and cooking. In fact, even more now that their husbands are home for three meals a day."

I'd seen what she was talking about. I remembered how women would come in and smile just being in the store. It really was a sight: cozy and special-like. Della always said if she had to spend all day in there, she wanted it nice. These women liked that, felt at home—a home they didn't have to take care of. So they'd pick up a few extra things like

cookies from England or a jam that weren't blackberry—
something different like quince or marmalade. I figured
those items reminded them of a time when they was young,
or a memory of a trip they took. And they'd rave about the
cheeses she carried—something besides that rubbery
Velveeta everyone cooked with. I used to like Velveeta, but
then Della had me taste other cheeses, and there was no
going back. I drew the line at some of them stinky ones, but
I missed the good cheeses when I went off to school. Just
thinking about them made my mouth water.

So those women would be all happy-like, or as happy
as they could get, until their husbands came in and right in
front of Della and me (when I was inside stocking shelves)
told them to put those nice things back. Like those women
were 10 year old. Some of them weren't even poor, like the
rest of us. More and more second-home people were
coming up from Knoxville or Asheville and even Atlanta.
They had money to burn. Man, it was so embarrassing for
everyone. And sad. I could never understand why their
husbands were being so hateful.

"Are they sittin' outside with Wilkie Cartwright and the
like?"

"No, that's what's killing me. They are *in the store* and
refuse to leave until I close up. They're having a strike of
sorts. Standing around, adding things to their baskets, and
just waiting for their hubbies to come and demand they put
them back on the shelves. Yesterday, that retired Marine
colonel came in and caused a real scene. Kathleen, his wife,
went straight to the register when he came in and plunked

down a twenty dollar bill. He tried to snatch it away, but she held firm. He grabbed her arm, roughly, and the other women swarmed around him, like Elbert's bees protecting the queen. He backed off, but who knows what happened when they got home.

"And they've helped me out a time or two when I had to run an errand. But it's getting old—even though business is up. Some of the women whose husbands aren't like that are coming in and shopping more. In solidarity, I guess. And what with all the baking in support of the strike—like your mother's—I'm selling more ingredients. But I'm ready for this to be over."

"I'da thought you'd support them."

"Support, yes. But an encampment in my store? Over the top. This is between them and their husbands. I never wanted to change their way of life."

"But your just being there's changed things." She didn't say anything, so I added, "Like when Mama put my new blue jeans in the washer with her white sheets by accident. Them sheets looked light blue from then on."

"Okay, I get your comparison. I'm a stain on their lives." I knew she was just being contrary, so I didn't explain myself. "But, you know, I can't do it *for* the women. This strike is only a surrogate for the changes they need to foment in their own lives. I want to support them, but they need to take this fight home."

"I don't hold by that."

"What are you talking about, Abit?"

Honestly, I wasn't sure. I didn't know what some of those words Della used even meant, but my gut was churning. "Well, you could say that about any situation. Like how they picked on me in elementary school. You could say that was just between me and the bullies. But you know it was bigger than that. Same here. You're a living, breathing example of another way to be. I reckon everything about you and the store is a slap in the face to the way their husbands think their wives should live."

Della went quiet for what felt like ages, and her tone had changed when she said, "Listen, Abit. You need to stay where you are. That helps me just knowing you're doing what you need to so you'll soon be going back to school. And I'll give some thought to what you just said. In the meantime, I hope this 'bigger' thing ends soon."

I couldn't find a place for the night, so I slept in the Merc. It had a wide backseat, and with the thick down sleeping bag Alex'd loaned me, I figured I'd be okay. But I couldn't get to sleep. I was reliving my call with Della and thinking about that strike. That store was a bright spot for some and a poke in the eye to others.

I tossed and turned a while, to the point I had to get out of the car and untangle the sleeping bag. While I was up, I pulled out my flashlight, got back in the sleeping bag, and opened Alex's con artist report. It wasn't the kind of reading that helped you fall asleep, but I wanted to know more about what I was up against.

I got to the part explaining a bunch of the cons like "The Play," "The Rope," and "The Hook." Clayne and Mama Mae combined all three to get the director—playing off the scarcity of affordable land. What with all the second-home people and weekend farmers from the city coming up and grabbing land, everything was getting more and more expensive. I couldn't've said how many times I'd heard Daddy complain it was a good thing we owned our home or we'd never've been able to afford to live there. Land round the school was going up and up in price, so the director was easy prey for a good deal. As for the dying mama, that played on everyone's emotions, and they fooled us all. Except for that time I caught Mama Mae without her diapers, they was smooth as silk. They mostly got chump change from us, but that set the stage for the big one (The Rope). And it wasn't chump change to us.

Then there was the fake-similarity con Clayne and Mama Mae played on Jewel. I felt sad remembering Jewel saying she felt "some fool loyalty to that young man" and how Mama Mae acted all reassuring about the peace of mind she got from that mortgage. That kind of loyalty also helped when anyone started trash talking them. Oncet marks believed in them—like us trying to help Mama Mae spend her final days near her so-called family home—we were more likely to ignore criticisms, even when they made sense.

Cons understood all too well how hard people stuck to their beliefs. I sure knew about that from all the years I sat in my chair outside Daddy's and then Della's store. Like if

Wilkie Cartwright came to believe that Big Foot lived in his holler, there was no budging him. Or Daddy—he thought I was stupid, and he'd hear no different. Those con artists played offa that kind of stubbornness.

I finally wore myself out and fell asleep, but I kept waking up wrestling with that blamed sleeping bag—and what lay ahead. Too often at night I'd feel a rush of dark thoughts that overwhelmed any good sense I had. What if I ran outta gas? What if I lost Nigel's pictures? What if *I* got lost? Stupid things that by the light of day didn't seem so bad.

About four o'clock, I gave in to being awake and started appreciating the quiet. I'd never been in the heart of the night, alone with just a thin wall of steel and glass between me and it. Through the windshield, I could see millions of stars, in spite of the gibbous moon, and felt grateful there were no clouds. I couldn't recall ever feeling so much stillness.

After a while, something shuffled out of the woods into the clearing where I'd parked. At first, I couldn't make out what it was, but then the white on its back glowed in the moonlight. I watched that skunk scurry in front of the Merc and make its way across the clearing. The mist had started to rise, swirling round him and cutting him off from everything else, until he looked like the only creature left on earth.

When I was a kid, I always wanted a skunk hat—like Daniel Boone's except with the white stripe down the middle and the black-and-white tail hanging down. I asked

Ernie, a local guy who fooled with taxidermy, if he'd make me one. Not kill the skunk, but make it from roadkill I could find most any day of the week. He told me no way. The stink would stay with that hat forever, following that skunk well beyond the grave. That made sense to me. I knew all about things following you no matter where you went.

Chapter 17

"Who the hell are you?" the black-haired man asked after rolling out from under his truck. At first I thought oil had dripped on his face, but then I realized he had such dark bushy eyebrows, they looked like a couple of caterpillars had camped out on his forehead. I was trying not to stare at them when he growled his unwelcome at me.

Earlier that morning, I'd had trouble pulling myself out of the Merc after that lousy night's sleep. That backseat might've been okay if I were 8 year old and a foot shorter, but not in my current state. Oncet I got out, I stretched a time or two to ease my back and neck, then folded myself into the front seat and cranked the engine. I was starving.

Within a few mile, I found a diner with a sign flashing OPEN. A waitress showed me to my table, and then I headed to the restroom to clean up. I looked in the mirror and felt like a fool when I saw all the creases on my face from sleeping on the upholstery. One or two looked like bad scars, which made my scruffy beard look even worse than it already did. (I'd decided to let my beard grow since I couldn't count on a good place to bathe or shave.) I brushed my teeth and headed back to breakfast.

I treated myself to the special—short stack, two eggs over easy, bacon, and coffee. After all that (but just one cup of coffee—not sure what happened to the waitress), I made my way south. I started thinking about what I'd read last night and wondering why those cons had singled me out and put money *into* my account. I mulled that over for a good twenty mile. Not long after, I saw a sign for Wades Tavern, where Nadine said Burlon had a cousin named Luther.

I wished I'd asked if Luther was related to the dead one. I didn't want to go barging in again on someone who was having fond family memories. Funerals did that to folks, remembering the good stuff and forgetting most of the bad. I drove into his yard and noticed some feet sticking out from under an old Ford truck, lacy with rust round its fenders. That's when he rolled out and started waving, friendly-like. But before I could even get out of the car, he barked his "Who the hell are you?" at me, just like his cousin Burlon had the day before.

"Who'd you think I was?" I asked.

"Well, not that it's any of your business, but I thought you were my mother. She drives a car a lot like yours."

"Hey, lucky her. Does hers make as much noise as mine?"

"Yeah, that diesel engine can really ... oh, to hell with that. What do you want?"

His eyes below them caterpillars looked mean as Burlon's. Small black centers that nearabout bore a hole through me. "I'm looking for some folks." I held up Nigel's drawings, and the man's face changed faster than weather in October.

"We'd better talk," he said.

I guessed misery does love company, because in spite of our shaky start, pretty soon Luther and I were talking up a storm. He wiped his hands on a dirty rag and asked, "You want to come over to the house for some coffee?"

That gave me a funny feeling, but I figured it was a flashback to Steve Thompson, the coffee-enema guy. He said those very words one day when he asked me to stop by and meet his wife. I wanted to ask him how he was *serving* that coffee. He did use cups, but I never felt comfortable sippin' it. I'd always been a visual kinda guy.

I shook off that memory and said yes. After that rough night and stingy waitress, I needed some. It was good and strong, perked atop his woodstove. Which was cranking out more heat than I liked, but it was turning cooler outside and the wind was picking up, so he musta been getting a head start on the chill.

While I drank my first cup, I started to share my tale of woe, though something told me to make out like they'd stolen money from me. Luther listened carefully, and oncet I finished, he just nodded, like he'd heard it all before. I asked if I could help myself to more coffee, and he nodded again.

When I sat back down, he asked more questions about where I was headed next and what I planned to do if I found them. I played down what I really wanted to do—turn them over to the law—and just said I wanted my money back. I didn't like all his questions, so I turned the tables on him and asked about his family.

He seemed to enjoy telling me about Mama Mae—how she was originally from southern Virginia, a place called Damascus. She was a wild thing growing up and hooked up with a string of fellows. They were mostly no counts, and one of them was Clayne's daddy. (No one was sure which one.) After the last one got sent up the river for almost killing someone, she moved somewhere in the eastern part of the state and raised her boy. No other sons or daughters, which confirmed that Clarice wasn't Clayne's sister.

Mama Mae became a grifter, Luther said, to have enough money to raise her boy. He recalled what a good storyteller she was, and a smile split his face when he started telling how she conned a preacher and took off with that Sunday's collection plate. He had me laughing, but then I caught myself. That showed why she was so good at what she did. It was too damn easy to get caught up in her tales.

"Any idea where they might be right now?" I asked.

"Well, they stay on the road a good bit, going to out-of-the-way places, like where you met them. Hard to say."

"Where do they call home?"

"That's just it, they don't. They try to stay a step or two ahead of the law, so there's no telling." Then he started talking about his family tree and how, while they had crooks in that tree, they also had lawmen. One of his brothers worked in Charlottesville as a detective and a cousin down round Bristol was a sheriff. He carried on, but I didn't mind because while he talked, he started pulling food out of the fridge and pantry, including some sliced ham, a fat loaf of bread, and apple hand pies he said he'd made himself.

Looked mighty good, though a sick feeling came over me that he might be fattening the pig for slaughter. But I'd gone through just about everything Della packed, and I needed to watch my money.

When I'd finished eating, Luther mentioned how he'd worked on his mama's Merc, and he could help me cut down on the racket. I flashed on what Jewel had said, and said sure, but I didn't have any money to pay him.

"Listen, after what my cousins did to you, it's the least I can do." He slapped me on my back and headed outside.

I grabbed another hand pie and tucked it in my pocket for later. To pay him back, I started clearing up and doing the dishes. While I washed, I thought about how I felt as uncomfortable about kindness as I did about meanness. That struck me odd, something to think about on the long ride ahead.

A heavy fog came over my brain after that big lunch, especially since I hadn't slept good the night before. I drove a while, thinking I'd come round, but I couldn't shake it. I pulled the Merc off the highway when I saw a sign for a county park and stopped under a shady poplar tree so bright yellow it should've kept me awake. It didn't. Some kids hollerin' woke me, and I sat up and watched them play just like the kids back home in the schoolyard. I started imagining how their lives were—hoping they had nice parents and were doing good in school. Something about that scene gave me new feelings of hope—even happiness.

I wasn't sure why or what that was about, but I liked it. I reached for that hand pie from Luther's that was sitting on the dashboard in the sun. I celebrated my good feelings with a warm pie in the Merc—*my* Merc—and at that moment felt like the King of Sheba.

I cranked the car and headed toward Marionville, where the next mark lived. Seemed Ila Pittman had complained to the police about a trio of cons who'd taken her for $500. Even $500 could set somebody back for months. Alex found her by reading a brief news articles in the *Lexington News-Gazette*, which he noted in his report for me. Ever since he got in trouble back when he worked for the *Washington Post*, he identified everything he found real careful-like.

And just like Luther promised, as I drove south, the car rode quieter. That made me feel easier, knowing the Merc wouldn't stand out so much.

Chapter 18

I got mad and sad all over again at Ms. Pittman's. Her story sounded pretty much like the rest of the Ledbetters' victims I'd talked to, so I didn't really learn anything new. But it still pissed me off that they'd screwed such a nice person. I knew I needed to work on hiding my anger so I didn't scare these folks, especially some of the women who were already trembly as they shared their sorrows.

While I had the chance, I asked Ms. Pittman about the handmade sideboard in her dining room—one of the prettiest I'd ever seen. She was real pleased I'd asked because her dead husband had made it for her when they first married. She jumped up and pulled it away from the wall (with strength that surprised me), so I could take a closer look at the dovetail joints he'd made. I spent a good ten minutes studying the wood and careful details of a fine craftsman. After we'd pushed it back in place, I thanked her for her time and promised I'd let her know if I found out anything that could help her. I doubted I could live up to that, but I meant what I said.

One thing that killed me—even though Clayne was such a shithead, the women he picked on always mentioned how handsome and nice he was. And they even seemed to like that sickly aftershave he wore. I had a hard time seeing that. All I could think of was what he'd taken from me and all the others. And the ugly looks he always sent my way.

When I drove off, I headed toward Bennettsville. Before long, I noticed the sun was just hitting the treetops. I'd let the night creep up on me (easy to do late in October), and it would be dark in no time. I didn't know these roads, especially at night, but I figured I'd push on a ways since I had the road to myself.

Until I didn't.

After a mile or two, I noticed some lights behind me, but I didn't give that much thought till the vehicle started speeding up and slowing down whenever I did. That wasper feeling started up again. When I got to a straightaway, I floored the accelerator until I reached a spot where I couldn't see any headlights behind me. I cut my lights and pulled off the road, crawling along a rutted path, careful not to hit my brakes to keep the red lights from flashing. I drove a ways farther and stopped.

My heart was racing so hard I had trouble breathing. I forced a few big breaths to try to calm myself. Then I saw a pickup drive past—white, I think, though it was hard to tell in the fading light. I rolled down my window to help me study the situation and waited. Just when I was thinking I musta spooked myself, sure enough, that truck went by again, real slow-like, in the opposite direction. About ten minutes later, he came back by and pretty soon I heard him shout, "Shit!" followed by a shotgun blast I hoped was pointing toward the sky. He turned his truck round, gunned it, and burned rubber.

I waited another ten minutes to make sure I was alone. Only a small dark car went by, making its way back the other direction, away from Bennettsville. The same way the white truck was headed, which gave me some peace of mind.

As I sat there surrounded by nothing but the dark, something came over me, the likes of which I'd never felt before: *I really wanted to live.* Most of my life, I'd been lurking in the shadows, but I'd finally stepped into the daylight, and I wasn't about to let some con artists take that away from me. I wanted to learn to do something that mattered, the best I could. And have a dog of my own—maybe even get married someday. All them things shot through my mind in a flash.

I stayed there a while longer, still scared to death but appreciating what I was thinking. When I figured the coast was clear, I took another deep breath and started the Merc. I drove down into Bennettsville, looking for a place for supper. These small towns all seemed alike to me, not much different from Laurel Falls in that they usually had a general store, a beauty/barber shop, and a café. We had a few more shops back home since we were considered a tourist stop. The falls really are that pretty.

I worried that the café would be out of everything, but my luck was holding. While I worked my way through some pretty good chicken and gravy, I asked my waitress if she knew Marcus Frye, the next guy on Alex's list. She looked a little surprised, and I asked her why.

"Because I don't know why a nice boy like you'd be lookin' for him."

I wasn't concerned about his character as much as any clues he might have about Mama Mae's whereabouts, but I was also feeling wore out. I was about to tell her never mind when I recalled my revelation. I forced myself to ask where I might find him.

She looked at her watch and said, "He's likely at his repair shop, just a couple blocks down this street," pointing behind me.

I figured car and truck repair in these parts must be a booming business. Nobody could afford a new one, so all them old ones relied on shade-tree mechanics like Luther and Marcus to keep them running. As I walked thataway, I saw a payphone and decided to call Della.

Wednesday was Rollin' Store day, and I was dying to know how things were going. Back before I went off to school, Duane Dockery and I wound that old school bus through the hollers to bring folks fresh food and canned goods. Della always gave me stuff from the store that weren't selling so good, and I loved passing them out, watching the delight folks got from a gift so small. I hoped the Rollin' Store was doing okay without me. When I first left for school, they retired it for a while, but a few months ago, Duane talked Della into starting it up again. (Della also retired my chair—the one I'd always sat in outside the store—and hung it in the back of the store, high up on a nail on the wall. She told she was keeping it safe, but assured me I was always welcome at the store.)

After we said our howdy-dos, I told her about meeting Luther. "He fed me and shared some background on them three. And I confirmed that Clayne and Clarice weren't sister and brother."

"Well, Mister, those three are awfully good at making up stories and conning people." She was just trying to make me feel better.

"Yeah, well, I already knew that. Oh, and Luther's a mechanic. He fixed the Merc so it doesn't make such a racket."

"That's good," she said, then added, "I guess."

I was surprised she'd said that, given how much she hated the noise that car made. "Yeah, be sure and tell Alex it's fixed." She promised she would.

We chatted some more, and I asked about the Rollin' Store. "It's doing great. Cleva Hall started riding along with Duane to replace you." My heart cramped so bad I mighta made a noise. Della musta heard because real quick-like she said, "Abit, I'm sorry. That came out all wrong. You could *never* be replaced. Duane told me the folks are always asking about you. I should have mentioned that first thing. But Duane needed some help, and Cleva began to feel closed up, living all alone out in the boonies. A lot of people get that way after the first rush of retirement wears off, especially when they live so far out of town. She loves getting out and visiting with folks she hasn't seen in years."

"Why'd Duane feel lonely? He always told me he liked to drive to get away from all that family mess."

She paused for what felt like forever. "Honey, I hate telling you this on the phone, but he and Mary Lou are getting a divorce."

"Shit! I thought they was working things out."

"They tried, but sometimes things don't go the way we want."

"But you and Alex seem to have worked things out." I knew that was dumb as soon as I said it, as if that meant everyone could do that.

Della let it go. "Honestly, they both seem happier."

I didn't feel happier. Duane was all alone, their kids didn't have a regular daddy anymore, and I'd been replaced. I felt so damn sad, what with all this bad news and me out here on the road to nowhere. We hemmed and hawed for a while, and then Della said, "Call me tomorrow at the store, if you want, or after dinner," she said. "I should be around— and maybe I'll have some better news." She said bye and hung up.

I'd been away at school almost four year, so I was used to not seeing Della every day. It'd been hard at first, but I'd gotten used to it. And I spent a fair amount of time with her on the weekends when I came home, helping out in the store on Saturdays, sometimes for free. She tried to pay me, but I told her to forget that. I owed her plenty. Besides, these were just odd jobs I did so I could hang out with her. But these phone calls were getting to me. It stung to hear about life going on so good without me.

I was wallowing in those sorrows when I realized how late it was getting. I needed to find somewhere to stay the night—I couldn't face that backseat again. The town wasn't big enough to get lost in, and I quickly found a tourist home one street over. The woman at the desk stood tall and straight as a tulip poplar, giving me the once-over. I'd combed my hair, and I felt good about my clothes, even if they were kinda rumpled after a long day in the Merc. And my beard had grown in enough I didn't look like a vagrant no more. I stood at attention, putting on my best behavior because I didn't want her turning me down. I musta passed because she stuck out her hand to shake and introduced herself as Mrs. Meldau, the owner and cook. But she still made me pay in advance.

Her home was like something out of an antiques catalogue, though I doubted anything was all that valuable. Just old. She had some of them lamps that looked like oil lamps—two globes, one atop the other—but they were electric. Lace curtains on the windows, doilies on the couch, everything spic and span. Mama woulda loved it.

I asked how late the front door was open, since I had a little business to take care of. She raised an eyebrow, but then just nodded and handed me a key. "$10 if you lose it."

I took the stairs to my room, plunked my grip on the bed, and headed out again. I made my way in the direction my waitress had pointed—but the only building nearby was Logan's Roadhouse. I'd wondered why she'd made little marks in the air with her fingers when she said "repair shop," and now I got it. Oncet inside, I saw several men huddled at the end of the bar and some at individual tables. They all turned to stare at me.

I sidled up to the bar and ordered a beer. I didn't want it, but I'd seen too many TV westerns where some greenhorn orders a sarsaparilla and everyone laughs at him.

The bartender didn't even ask for ID. I sipped at the beer, trying to look casual-like. The jukebox played some country song with some sad-sounding man belting out, "You took me partway to somewhere, but it looks like nowhere from here." I knew that feeling, all right.

I asked the bartender if Marcus Frye was there. He said he was out of town, then turned toward a couple at the other end of the bar. Not long after that, one of the men sitting at a nearby table took the stool next to me. "Whatcha doing in Bennettsville, kid?"

"Oh, just passing through."

"That right? We might've heard different."

"That right?" I said, my tone coming out sharp-like, but really I was just scared shitless.

"Yeah, that's right. We heard you've been showing pictures around to folks in the area, stirring up some bad feelings."

"Oh, I didn't stir up bad feelings. They were already there. When someone steals your savings and you get thrown out of your house, those feelings don't need no stirring." I could feel heat rising up my neck.

"Well, you be careful, ya hear?"

I sipped my beer as I strained to hear what he was telling the others back at their table. I felt like a hen in a fox's den, so I figured it was time to go. As I slipped off the barstool, I heard their chairs scraping the wood floor. Four of them. That was when I started running to the Merc. I could hear them shouting at me as I tried to crank the car. Only it wouldn't. I tried again, grinding the starter and straining to lock the passenger-side door, only to see it fly open.

Chapter 19

I woke face down in a puddle. I musta blacked out, but as I started to come to, I heard voices that sounded like a 45 record played at 33-1/3.

"We should kick this bastard into the creek," a man with a deep voice said before he acted out part of his plan with a swift kick to my butt. Fortunately, he hit the part with the most padding, so I didn't give away I was awake.

"What's he got on ya?" a squeaky voice asked.

"Nothin', stupid. I just didn't like him asking around about family."

Even with my eyes closed, I sensed headlights—and help coming our way. "We gotta go, Clayne," Squeaky Voice said.

Someone kicked me again, this time in the ribs, and kinda growled, "Listen here, you dumb shit, mind your own business. Go home!"

I lay there what felt like forever, long after I heard their footfall fade and that car splash past me. I finally opened my eyes and looked round, though it hurt like crazy just to move my eyes. My head throbbed, and I saw that my clothes were all muddy. And that I wasn't where I thought I was. They musta carried me somewhere while I was out.

I brushed myself off best I could. I felt my head and looked at my hand. My head wasn't bleeding, at least not anymore. But the Merc was nowhere round. As I started walking, I limped from a bad pain in my hip.

While I searched for my car, I felt a chill come over me that had nothin' to do with the night air. Loud and clear, I heard Squeaky Voice use the name Clayne. Now that ain't a common name, at least not in my world, so I knew the odds. And he talked about "family." If it was him, he musta joined them after they stole me away from the bar, because I woulda recognized his pretty face as soon as I'd walked into the bar.

My heart started hammering when I thought about Clayne—and likely Mama Mae and Clarice—being nearby, and I had to stop to steady myself. Then Luther came to mind. It hurt to think how he'd acted all buddy-buddy with me, but he was just pumping me for information. Another con in the family. He'd screwed up my car, and I'll bet he'd called Clayne, knowing where I was headed next—and that I wouldn't get too far down the road before the car gave out.

After walking about a half mile (that felt like ten), I saw a church I remembered from my drive into town. I don't know why it caught my eye, probably the sign out front: "Mine Fields: The danger of selfish lives." I'd been thinking something like that the night before, wondering if this whole crazy trip was just selfish on my part. Revenge, even. But then I figured I had a right to defend myself, and since the cops weren't doing nothin', someone needed to help the folks they'd conned—and were fixin' to con.

Which was what I had to keep telling myself as I wandered into town, limping now worse than old man Cunningham, one of our World War II vets back home. I sighed with relief when I came up on the Merc sitting in front of Mrs. M's, broken down right where I'd left it. I felt round all my pockets for the front door key and considered myself $10 richer that it hadn't fallen out during the fight.

The next day, I woke up feeling like the devil, and one of my eyes had swole up in a scary way. I had to spend another day in Bennettsville, because one, I wasn't about to go calling on strangers lookin' like that, and two, the Merc needed fixin'. But I was also wrestling with this strange battle going on inside—yes, I wanted to catch Clayne, and yet he scared me enough that I wanted to get as far away from him as I could. The two didn't work together, so I needed to pick one or the othern.

One comfort I took was, based on the stories I'd heard and what I knew firsthand, Clayne was so full of himself, he probably figured he'd scared me away. He wouldn't be looking for me, as long as I was smart about who I talked to next. But that posed another problem, because I'd worked my way through Alex's list with only a couple more to go. I hoped they could direct me to folks who weren't too scared or old to speak up when I finally swore out a complaint. And weren't their family!

I didn't want breakfast, especially looking the way I did, so I lay in bed thinking about Clayne and how he'd acted at The Hicks. I knew in my heart that he hated me not just because I was looking for him. I reckoned one of those kicks was for kissing his wife. But you couldn't run a con and get mad when someone fell for it. Then again, I guessed you could.

I hurt so bad I felt like crying, which reminded me of the time Clayne was bawling his eyes out over his Mama Mae, so sad that she was dying. We were all at a fundraiser for them, and Clayne got up to play his guitar and sing "Rank Stranger," but he broke down halfway through the song. Mama Mae got teary eyed, too, but motioned for him to keep a-going. There weren't a dry eye in the place, and money was flowing into the coffee cans they were passing round. At the time, everyone was all, "Oh, that poor boy ..." Me included.

That memory made me so mad, just thinking about how they worked us all over, that I got up and got dressed. Besides, my appetite had come back. I'd missed Mrs. M's breakfast—served *sharply* at seven o'clock, she'd said— and somehow it didn't feel right going back to last night's diner, even though that waitress had only pointed out what I'd asked for. Still, I worried that everyone was connected. Good thing I'd spotted another café not far off the main street.

Mrs. M was at the bottom of the stairs, and she looked at me like Mama used to when I'd get into some kind of a scrape. I knew she probably figured I'd been in a barroom brawl. As I scooted out the front door, I mentioned that I needed to stay another night. She just shook her head and told me I wasn't to start any trouble.

I walked to the café slowly because I was stiff and sore. But to be honest, I was already kinda milking the limp. Like the way Wilkie'd told me oncet after he'd sprained his ankle, he knew it was getting better when he couldn't remember which leg to limp on.

The day had turned cold and dark, but for some fool reason I felt happy. I was a million miles from home, thrown outta school, aching inside and out, and yet life seemed good. It wasn't till I turned down McCallum Street, heading for that other café, that it hit me.

I'd passed.

Passed as just another fellow human being. Nothing to write home about, but also not a retard, jerk, or pansy—or any of the other names I'd been called all my life. No one, not Jewel or Nadine, not Burlon or Luther, not even Clayne talked down to me that a-way.

I'd passed!

Lucky for me there was a bench out front of the café, because I needed to sit down. "I passed," I said out loud.

I thought of Jewel and her evening gratitude offerings, and I paused there on the bench to offer one about going to The Hicks and getting help with the way I thought about myself. A counselor there explained how there were all kinds of ways to screw up a kid's head. She told me that what folks had said to me most my life contributed to my so-called slowness because they brainwashed me into believing it, too. I knew I was getting better and doing pretty darned good in school, but I hadn't figured that folks would treat me just like anyone else in the world. And, more to the point, that even Clayne saw me as a worthy opponent.

The sun suddenly broke through the clouds. As I put on my sunglasses, I realized my eyes and face were soaking wet. And you know what? I didn't care. Not a lick. I wiped my face, ran my fingers through my hair, and opened the café door. I was starving.

It looked like a hole in the wall, but the smoked pork with sweet potatoes and biscuits hit the spot. I took a chance and asked my waitress, Bonnie, if she knew a good mechanic in town. Turned out her brother, Mike, had a small shop within walking distance. He towed the Merc, and by late afternoon I confirmed that that bastard Luther had monkeyed with my exhaust. Mike said I was lucky it didn't die on me in the middle of nowhere—or poison me to death.

While Mike fixed the Merc, I headed over to the post office to get a plain postcard to send home to Mama. (I didn't figure she'd look at the postmark.) I wrote the usual stuff about the weather and school and such while I hung out at the café, drinking coffee and trying not to watch the TV mounted on the wall. (Something about a TV draws me to it like yellow jackets to a picnic.) After a while, the news came on, and I caught a story about a storytelling festival coming up in Duncan Mills, somewhere a good bit south, according to Bonnie. I loved a good story. I was weaned on 'em, what with all them guys on the bench out front of the store—Daddy included—who could spin yarns that had you laughin' or cryin' or both. I would've liked to go, but I figured I'd better stick to my plan. Besides, I'd already taken a couple of days off because I looked like a prizefighter who didn't get the prize.

By the time I got back to Mrs. M's, she was pulling supper out of the oven. I quickly cleaned up and came back down to join two other guests—a traveling tire salesman and a teacher who came about a job opening. Mrs. M filled the table with meatloaf and potatoes and green beans and dinner rolls. Turned out, I liked her meatloaf better than Mama's because it didn't have all those gross green peppers in it. Hackbraten, she called it. A German dish, she said, which made sense given her husband, Ernie, spoke with a strong German accent. It wasn't so great to look at, but the carrots and onions plus the meatloaf with sour cream on top tasted awfully good with the mashed potatoes. And fresh apple pie a la mode for dessert.

I thought about heading down the road to the payphone, but I didn't want to go anywhere near that damned roadhouse. I asked Mrs. M if I could call Della collect.

"Della?" I said, after she'd told the operator she'd accept the call. "Thanks for accepting the charges."

"Oh, sure, honey. Anytime. And before I forget, Alex has been stewing about that so-called car repair and doesn't feel good about it. He said ..."

"I know. Do I ever know!" I interrupted. "That's what I was fixin' to tell you." I didn't know what else to say, because I didn't want to tell her about getting beat up. I brought her up to date on the car repairs, making out like Luther'd just done a bad job. But she musta heard somethin' in my voice.

"Abit, what's wrong?"

"Oh, everything's fine, now. In fact, something really good happened. I passed."

"You heard from the school?"

"No, not that kind of passed. I passed, you know, as a regular person." There was a long pause and my heart kinda froze up. I waited a while longer and added, "Della, you don't believe me?"

"No, honey, that's not it. I didn't realize that you didn't already know that. You've always passed. It's just the idiots around you who didn't know."

Like I'd said before, kindness got to me more than meanness. I switched the conversation round by asking how the brouhuhu was shaping up.

"Brouhaha. And there's nothing ha-ha about it. We're at a stalemate. No one's budging. The women still come every day, and the men show up later and stand near the register, glaring at their wives. It's the craziest thing I've ever seen."

"Crazier than Blanche Scoggins?" Blanche was the wild woman who owned the local laundromat and hated everyone who used it.

"Yes, if you can believe it."

"Man, them guys—the husbands—can be so mean. I saw it with my own eyes. Any other news?"

"Sheriff Brower has a new girlfriend. She seems pretty nice, too. She stops by for this and that, and I've enjoyed chatting with her."

"How do these guys do it? They've got beer guts and act like jerks, but they get the girls."

"Hey, that's my line," Della said, laughing. "I don't know. Maybe they're better than nothing. Life can get pretty lonely."

"Tell me about it. I'm out here in the middle of nowhere, and not a friend in the world."

"Not a friend there *with* you, you mean."

"Okay, I know you and Alex are rooting for me, but ..."

"And Cleva and Duane and Mary Lou and ..."

"Say, how's Duane doin'?"

"He's doing fine with the rolling store. Cleva says he's pleasant with her and all the customers. But I know it's hard going through a divorce. You have good days and not so good."

"Tell him I said hi. And Cleva, too. I don't reckon Mary Lou is part of the strike, is she? I mean without Duane, nobody's tellin' her not to buy what she wants."

"Well, you know, he never did *that* to her. Maybe they can work it out, after all. He's got some heavy lifting to do, and I guess she does, too, but who knows?"

We both paused a moment, and I was afraid our conversation was about over. If only it had been.

"And, uh, Abit, one more thing. Watch out for your grammar. Your hard-earned progress has taken a tumble since you've been hanging out with the likes of those Jewels and Nadines."

And just like that, I hung up on her. Earlier on, she'd said some really kind things to me, but that dig about them women just cut right through me. It hurt to hear her talking that way about two of the nicest people on my trip—and she'd never even met them. And I was sick of people telling me how I oughta be—and tired of thinking I had to jump at all their suggestions. It just felt good to shut her up.

Until it didn't. As I cooled off, I realized she probably wasn't being snotty—just looking out for me. But still, that comment stung.

I thought about calling her back, but I couldn't bring myself to calling her collect again. What if she refused the charges? I went up to my room and lay on the bed, running over our phone call, trying to figure out how it went so wrong.

After a while, I rolled over to look on the nightstand at the books guests had left behind. I wondered if I could get through any of them; my reading skills still weren't the best. One of them kinda jumped out at me—*Ladder of Years* by Anne Tyler. I started reading, and the story grabbed me when this woman, Delia, left behind a life she didn't want to live anymore. Riding down a highway, not knowing where she was going, just like me. I didn't know what every word meant, but I felt a strong kinship with her. I was struck, too, by how her name was just one letter off from my best friend's. Maybe former best friend's.

After an hour or so, when Delia was busy settling into her new home, I needed some fresh air. That meatloaf smell hung in the well-insulated house like a skunk's spray. I stepped outside and settled on the back stoop. I'd parked the Merc in the back so those bastards wouldn't see it out front.

As I sat there, admiring the starry sky, I saw a cop shining a light into the Merc. Oh, crap. Just what I didn't need.

I scurried over to an old shed and hunkered down, hoping the cop would move on. He did—in my direction. I pressed myself flat against the shed, but next thing I knew, that damned flashlight was blinding me.

"Are you V.J. Bradshaw?"

"Yee-es, sir."

"Just the man I'm looking for."

Chapter 20

Deputy Jenkins showed me a newspaper story where his mama, Era Head Jenkins, told her sad story about Billy Ray and Mary Grace taking nearabout $4,000 from her. I knew those were aliases for Clayne and Mama Mae because their M.O. was all over it.

"She's old, and it nearly killed her," he said, taking his hat off out of respect, like you see people do on TV at funerals.

The article was just in a small local paper, but the reporter wrote a good story, trying to help Mrs. Jenkins out. But nothing came of it. That was why Deputy Jenkins looked me up when he heard I was hunting them three. I knew how news traveled fast in small towns, and this time, it worked in my favor.

"Why won't the cops or law people do anything?" I asked. We'd moved to the steps in front of Mrs. M's. (She looked out just then, and when she saw a cop talking to me, I swear I could hear her tongue clucking, even through the closed window.)

"Not enough folks coming forward. Law enforcement has a limited budget, and a case has to have teeth—enough to warrant the time and money. I'd bet these three are feeling cocksure; they'd never expect anyone to come after them, certainly not a young man like you." I'm not sure what he meant by that, but I let it go. "But word is spreading about you. Jewel Johnston told my mother. They know each other up in Staunton, where my mother lives, and that's how I heard about you. So you'd better be careful, especially with that car of yours."

That again. After Mike fixed the Merc, the rattle was back, but at least it was reliable again (though Deputy Jenkins' caution kinda scared me all over again). We sat there and talked a while, and he chuckled when he shared what his mama said about Clayne and Clarice. "I'll tell you," he said in a high, wavery voice, imitating her, "those two kids all lovey-dovey and all over one another. I just wanted to smack 'em.'"

I knew the feeling. Of course, they didn't play that act with me. I mean, even back in the hollers they wouldn't behave that a-way in public, not as brother and sister. But I sure wanted to smack 'em, too. At least Clayne. "Why didn't she just tell them to get outta her house and get a room?"

He laughed again. "Well, truth of it is, I think those two probably just hugged each other when she agreed to sign up for his reverse mortgage swindle. My mother is a real prude, so even the least little affection is tantamount to doing *it*."

That made me laugh for the first time in days—at the way people referred to sex as *it*. And there was never any question what they was talking about. I musta laughed a little too hard because Deputy Jenkins looked at me funny. I told him it was my nerves, but really what got me so tickled, even more than *it*, was I'd just realized his mama's maiden name was Era Head. It was just like a mountain mama to name her baby girl something like that, spelling it the best she could. Like a woman I knew back home whose name was Azalea Bush, though she pronounced is az-ah-LEE-ah. Anyways, I got myself under control and told Deputy Jenkins I wanted to talk with his mama. I guessed I wasn't running away from Clayne, after all.

"She's not doing too well. She's told me all about it, but swears she'd never testify against them. She trusts me to do whatever I can to help."

"They sure seem to pick on old people."

"Oh, they're equal opportunity destroyers. But yeah, old people are easier." He frowned then and added, "Look, I appreciate what you're doing, but you're just a kid. I wouldn't be doing my job if I encouraged you to keep after these criminals."

I didn't mention that I was 20 year old; somehow, I didn't think that would impress him. But I did tell him that nobody else was doing anything, and I was up to my ears in the problems they'd caused me, like being thrown out of school and off on this crazy trip. He nodded and patted me on the back. We sat quiet for a while before he said, "Here's my card. When you find out anything solid about these crooks, get in touch. I know a lot of law enforcement around the state, so I can come or get someone closer by to help out. I think you're going to need it."

Chapter 21

I was back on the road early after I'd settled up with Mrs. M. While I was at it, I'd asked if I could pay for *Ladder of Years*. I wanted to finish that story, and since it was a nice hardback book, I didn't feel right just taking it. But she told me she didn't read much, so I was welcome to it. No charge. I wanted to hug her (I hadn't hugged anyone in ages), but something about her German ways made me hold off.

The day didn't pan out the way I'd hoped. The first person I visited lived just outside of Bennettsville and didn't know what I was talking about. Alden Martin, the next guy, nodded when I showed him Nigel's drawings, but when he told me about his woes, they were just like the rest. I didn't learn anything new.

After that, I headed to the town of Dillard. Along the way, I saw a hitchhiker and thought for a minute about breaking all the rules that'd been drummed into me and picking him up. No telling what might happen and where that could lead. But by the time I played out all those scenes in my head, I'd passed him.

I drove round Dillard and eventually found Doyle Nichols' trailer. Doyle didn't seem the least bit embarrassed about the con he'd fallen for. I was pretty sure it wasn't the work of Clayne and Mama Mae, and when I showed him their pictures, he just shook his head. But that didn't stop him from bending my ear. I didn't mind. The night before,

I'd read in Alex's report about the Pigeon Drop, and I wanted to hear about one from a real mark.

It all started with a shabby-looking guy coming into the diner where Doyle was the manager. He ate a big meal, from soup to ribeye steak to banana cream pie. When it came time to pay, he claimed he'd left his wallet at the motel a couple blocks away. Doyle was about to call the cops when the guy said he'd leave his fiddle, which he had on him because it was so valuable he couldn't trust leaving it in the room. He took it out of the case to show Roger, who told him he was in a good mood that day (and not a day since!), so go ahead, but be quick about it.

In a few minutes, a nicely dressed woman came in and saw the fiddle and had a conniption. Nothing would do but for her to have it. It was an antique, she said. She told Doyle she was in that business and knew its value. She offered him $12,000, right there and then, and Doyle thought his ship had come in. He said he'd let her know in an hour, if she could come back. He didn't want her staying for lunch and seeing the owner of the fiddle because he figured she'd want to do business with him direct. So he told her that her lunch would be on the house when she came back, and they could take care of business then. When Shabby Man showed up, Doyle told him his lunch was on the house, and he'd give him $200 for the fiddle. He figured Shabby Man would jump at that, but he demanded $500. Doyle got him down to $475, which was about all Doyle had in his savings. He fixed the guy up with another piece of pie while he went off to get his money. When he returned, he handed the guy $475 in cash, took the fiddle, and waited. And waited. That woman never came back, of course. She and Shabby Man were long gone to their next mark while Doyle was stuck with a fiddle worth about $30.

In a way, I felt sorry for Roger, but then I reminded myself that he was all ready to rip off his "customer." His own greed got the better of him. No wonder some folks don't go to the law after getting conned.

Roger's story about steak and pie got me hungry, so I stopped for lunch at a diner on the road south. Cheeseburger and potato salad followed by pear cobbler. And plenty of coffee, since I planned to drive a good bit more.

Heading down Highway 11, I saw a signpost for a state park named Hungry Mother. That made me think of Mama, who I'd swear was never really hungry. I cain't remember her eating much, ever, which accounted for her string-bean appearance. She just seemed to put on those big meals for me and Daddy. That made me sad on so many counts. For one, all that hard work, day after day. (Daddy and I could both put it away. We almost never had leftovers.) And I wished she'd enjoyed her food as much as we did. Growing up, mostly all I heard was what *not* to do, but we were *supposed* to eat three meals a day. In fact, we needed to, and that was like the best gift, especially since we were lucky enough to have plenty of food on our table. Each meal was like a celebration. But not for Mama.

I drove south a while, and next thing I knew, I'd passed a big ole owl sitting high up in a tree. I'd just caught a glimpse of it as I drove past, so I turned round to get another look. (I'd been missing the bird walks at school.) As I approached the tree, I stopped the car and looked up at the branch he was sitting on. Only it wasn't a bird—just a gash in the tree where a limb had blown off. Even close up, I could see how it looked like an owl, but really, I was probably just hungry to see something beautiful instead of all the ugliness I kept coming up against.

I drove to the address some woman had left the day before at Mrs. M's front desk. When I asked Mrs. M to describe her, she shook her head and said she'd just seen the woman's backside as she closed the front door. At the time, I hadn't given the note much thought, but when I realized how few folks I had left on my list, I figured I'd better take a look. I opened a pretty lavender envelope with matching paper and read how she'd heard I was on the trail of some scoundrels. (Like Deputy Jenkins had said, word was spreading about me.) Seemed her daddy had been ripped off by three people about six months ago. That jibed with the timing of the Ledbetters being up this way before they headed down to North Carolina. She asked if I could meet with him at four o'clock any day, as that was when he got home from work.

Just after three o'clock, I followed her directions to his cabin in the woods. As I headed up his drive, I realized I was a good thirty minutes early. (I'd had no idea how long it would take me, so I'd allowed plenty of time.) I found a shady spot off to the side in a small grove of trees, pushed the driver's seat back, and planned to rest a while.

I hadn't closed my eyes for five minutes when I heard some gears grinding up the old road. The old fellow musta gotten off work early. I knew it would've been rude to jump out the minute he got home after a hard day's work, so I figured I'd wait till he got settled in before knocking on his door.

I could just make out the truck through the trees as it pulled up to the cabin. A white pickup with a dented back fender. The driver didn't stop out front but pulled the truck round back. As he came toward the front of the house, I could see his face. Clayne. Carrying a shotgun down next to his right leg. He went up the steps and inside the cabin. And I'd been thinking he'd washed his hands of me.

I couldn't believe I'd let that SOB get the better of me again. Well, he hadn't gotten me yet. Something had nudged me to get a head start, and I was grateful for that—and the fact I was pretty well hidden in the trees. I just hoped my car didn't reflect the sunlight and catch his eye. I got lucky again when the sun went behind a thick cluster of clouds.

I couldn't see much, but I figured his pasty white face was looking out the window, just enough to see me, but not enough that I'd see him when I was supposed to drive up at four o'clock. I fumed as I thought about Mama Mae buying that girlie envelope and writing out that ambush note. Honestly, this trip wasn't getting me anywhere other than in trouble—or worse.

My chest started aching, and I realized I'd been holding my breath. I let out a big sigh and waited. Eventually, the sun went behind the mountain and dark shadows began creeping over the lake and cabin. Just after six o'clock, that bastard came out and slammed the door real hard. I could swear I heard glass cracking. But at least no blast from his shotgun, this time.

I prayed he wouldn't see me as he pulled out from behind the cabin. Even though it was already dark outside, I ducked down to make sure *my* pasty white face didn't catch his eye. And like last time, I waited a good fifteen, maybe twenty minutes, before I hit the highway.

Man, I didn't know where to turn. Them bastards seemed to know where I was going before I did! And I began to wonder what the point was of nearabout killing myself so I could go back to a school where they treated me like shit. Okay, only some folks did that to me, but the more I thought about it, that school had a taint on it. I'd lost my money, at least for now; everyone thought I was a criminal; and that crooked director was still there. Laurel Falls was looking better and better. I could learn music and carving and woodworking on my own.

And just like that, I decided this crazy trip was over. I was heading home to North Carolina.

Chapter 22

In spite of my troubles, in spite of nearly being killed or at least beat up again, my appetite was just like those café signs flashing OPEN, OPEN, OPEN. I couldn't remember a time I'd turned down a good meal. (Maybe oncet when I got mad at Della a few years ago.) Not that I'd call what I had a good meal—I stopped at a grocery for some sandwich fixin's for supper and bought ice for the cooler—but it was good enough. The weather was holding out, not too cold yet, so I planned to sleep in the car and make do with the food I had on hand. I just wanted to eat, sleep, and drive. Home.

Something about that rush I had back at the cabin left me feeling spent. Not to mention I needed to do something I'd been dreading: call Della. I hadn't talked to her since I'd hung up on her, and it was weighing on me. I used the phone booth out front of the store, and I had my apology all ready when Alex answered. Dammit! I loved talking with him, but I needed to get square with Della. Alex said she was down in the store late, trying to get the brouhaha resolved. I didn't want to get into that with him, and I didn't want to tell him how tired, sore, and lonesome I was. But his radar was as good as ever.

"Hey, you sound different, Abit. Everything going okay?"

A big lump in my throat choked off my words. "Well," I finally managed, "I got beat up. Don't tell Della. She'd worry too much. I'm okay, but I still ache. My face isn't puffy anymore, at least."

"Oh, damn. What happened?"

I brought him up to date, spilling my guts, not like I'd planned at all. I started at the beginning and finished by telling him about almost getting ambushed at the cabin.

"Sounds like you've hit a nerve. Some of these relatives—especially that Luther character—are likely in on their cons. They seem to have a tight network that keeps Clayne posted on your whereabouts. I'm surprised—and sorry. I'd never have sent you out on this crazy trip if I'd known it would take this turn. Be careful, Abit, and watch your back."

That really scared me. Up till I got beat up, I was thinking I was just finding out information to turn over to the cops. Hopefully someone better than Sheriff Brower back home. (I didn't care if he had a nice girlfriend; he was still an asshole. He didn't help Della one iota when she found that poor dead girl, Lucy. And then she let him take a lot of the credit when the reporters came round after *she*'d solved the murder. But I had to give Della credit—she kinda owned Brower after that.)

"I don't know *how* to watch my back," I said. "I mean I check the review mirror, just like you taught me. But what would I do if they came after me?"

He gave me some tips like if I was in the car, I needed to try to get somewhere with people round. If possible, I shouldn't pull over till I was in front of a police station or a sheriff's office—or somewhere real public. "But never mind all that, Abit. Why not come on home? No shame in that. You've gotten a good start, and we can keep at it from here. It's not worth your getting hurt."

I said I'd think about that. I didn't want to tell him I was already heading home. Before we hung up, I remembered something else. "Oh, and Alex, tell Della I'm sorry."

"For what?"

"She'll know."

Chapter 23

I couldn't get Alex's warning out of my head.

After we talked, I put a heavy foot on the accelerator. I was making good time, when out of nowhere, a thunderstorm came rolling down the highway. It seemed to be following the opening that'd been carved for the road because it hung over me like a bad dream. The wind was blowing so hard, even that German tank I drove was getting pushed round the road. I needed to find a place to pull over for the night.

But then I'd hear Alex telling me to watch my back. I kept looking in the rearview mirror, and I got the creeps, thinking about people looking for me. I'd had them feelings before, but usually they were coming from my head. This time, the fear was coming from a deeper place. That made me change my mind about sleeping somewhere on a side road. I doubted Clayne would be out in this storm, but I knew I wouldn't sleep a wink between the roaring wind and my howling mind.

I had no luck finding a place to stay. After another mile or two, I came up on an old-fashioned neon sign: "Sunset Mountain Trailer Park." I slowed down and pulled the Merc into the driveway, cut the engine, and let out a big sigh. I was safe, but I felt like I'd hit rock bottom staying at a trailer park. I'd had some bad experiences with them, what with all the bullies at grammar school seeming to come from the two we had back home. Maybe that was because everybody was crammed too close together, trailers lined up like hen's teeth. They seemed to breed trouble, and I dreaded what I'd get into at this one.

I didn't like it, but it was late enough that I didn't have much choice. And it felt safer than being tucked into some cove. The office was shut, so I pulled the Merc forward into an empty site. Oncet the rain let up some, I got out real quiet-like and walked round the grounds to work the kinks out after so much driving and sitting.

I could tell the park had seen better days. A mix of permanent trailers and the traveling kind were pulled on to broken concrete pads; scrub pine and weeds made their way up through the cracks, reaching for whatever sunlight they could find. Strings of small light bulbs, now dark, crisscrossed from tree to tree, hanging over the driveway like a spider's web swinging in the wind. The loneliness of the place reminded me of old Westerns, especially when debris brought down by the storm skittered across the driveway like tumbleweeds.

I hurried back to the Merc and crawled in the backseat. I got into my sleeping bag and tried to get comfortable. I musta done, because next thing I knew, the sun was shining bright in a sky washed that special blue that always seemed to follow a storm. Everything smelled good—the pines in particular with a sharp but pleasant aroma, likely coming off all the branches torn down by the winds. (I could see lots of "owls" up in the trees.) By daylight, the place looked a lot better. I headed to the office.

"Howdy. How'd you sleep?" asked an old man with a neatly trimmed white beard and a face as wrinkled as one of them applehead dolls Mama used to make. I was worried he was gonna get after me, but he said, "No charge. Any port in a storm." He was chuckling when he added, "That was some weather last night."

"Hey, thanks. And yeah, that weather made me stop driving. I appreciate the shelter."

"Well, you provided the shelter. We had the parking place." He musta thought that was a real hoot, because he was laughing again. I'd always found laughter catching and joined him.

"The name's Hank, by the way. What can I do for you …?" The way he said it, I knew he wanted my name.

"V.J. V.J. Bradshaw. And I could use another night here." Now that I'd made up my mind to end this trip, I wanted a day of rest.

I paid, and Hank pointed out the washroom. On the way, some friendly folks nodded at me, saying *good morning* and *nice day*, those kinds of things. Simple as they were, that felt special. While cleaning up, I started worrying about what to have for breakfast. I figured I could get by with one of my sandwiches and maybe Hank had some coffee I could buy.

As I walked back to the Merc, I smelled bacon cooking and actually licked my lips, the way Jake always did before his breakfast. The aroma was coming from a shiny old Airstream trailer, where a man sat out front in an aluminum lawn chair. He was wearing a bandana and one earring, like a pirate. I was kinda scared at first; he reminded me of Roger Turpin, a really bad guy who was a member of a militia group back home. But then he called out in a friendly way, "Hey, are you new? Where's your trailer?"

"Well, I got lost and couldn't find no motel. I'm just in that car, over there."

"Yeah, not much around here. Where're you from?" I hesitated, and he sensed I wasn't ready to give him my life's story. "We're a pretty friendly crew here, though nobody goes messing into anyone's private affairs." He pulled on his earlobe, the one without an earring, and added, "How about we make a trade? You join us for breakfast, and we'll share stories—true or made up." By then, I realized he reminded me of Duane, if he was dressed up for Halloween. I smiled and sat down.

Turns out his name was Enrico DeLuca, and his wife, Liliana, made me not just bacon but also eggs, French toast, butter, real maple syrup—they were from Canada!—and percolated coffee, just like I drank back home.

The insides of their trailer was paneled with mahogany. Enrico saw me looking close at the wood and said, proud-like, "They don't make 'em like that anymore." He motioned toward their dining table, which he said made into a twin-sized bed. All round, there were cabinets for everything. Even bookshelves, which I could tell had straps to secure the books while they were on the road. I'd've loved to have a small home like that—one you could take anywhere you wanted to go.

After breakfast, we all went outside and talked a while longer. They told me they came south every fall and winter to get away from six-foot snowdrifts. I made out like I was just on a trip to visit some relatives living in Staunton. I remembered to pronounce it right, though I doubted folks from Canada would know or care about that.

"Ever fish?" Enrico asked, out of the blue.

"No, we live in the mountains."

"Don't you have lakes and streams?"

"Well, yeah, but we were more like hunters. Daddy and his people."

"No reason you can't learn."

"No, sir. I guess I'm just not so inclined."

"Don't know till you try. If I'd waited for my daddy to approve of everything I did, I reckon I'd be setting on a bench whittling instead of living here." I could feel my color rise; sitting on a bench and whittling *was* about all I did before I went back to school. But then he made the prettiest motion with his hand, like a swallow getting ready for the night, pointing out all the beauty that surrounded us. I followed his hand and sure enough, this was all a lot better than setting on a bench and whittling. "Let's go, then," he said, kissing Liliana and ushering me toward his truck.

That evening Liliana cooked up the freshest trout I'd ever eaten, using the lightest touch with the cornmeal. I'd even caught one of the trout. I couldn't say I took to fishing that much, but I enjoyed the company and conversation.

I'd just wiped my mouth after eating the last of the home fries and coleslaw when she asked if I'd like coffee to go with her chocolate cake. "I'd better hold off. Sleeping in the backseat works okay, but I sure don't want to risk drinking something that might keep me awake."

"Sleep right here," Enrico said, slapping the table. "Well, after we make it into a bed," he added, chuckling. He'd taken off his bandana, exposing a head as bald as a newborn. He'd removed his earring, too, and no longer looked like a pirate—just the friendly old man he was.

I looked at Liliana, and she nodded her approval. It was a treat to stay in such a warm place, and a little light overhead meant I could read for a while to unwind. Delia in *Ladder of Years* had made a whole new life for herself, and I wanted to find out how that worked out for her.

When I turned out my light, I had an easy time with gratitude. I was full up with it. But then I started worrying about what I was gonna do next. I'd come clean with Enrico while we were on his boat, telling him about what I was really up to, and I could tell those con artists made him angry. I figured even though we barely knew each other, he didn't like it when crooks took advantage of poor folks. And he got frustrated with me about dropping outta school. "School is the most important thing you can pursue," he told me, waving some bait at me. After that, we didn't say much. He seemed to be working out something in his head.

Lying there in the dark, I felt uneasy. Just because I'd decided to give it all up, that didn't mean I was safe; Clayne or his buddies could still be after me. Fortunately, I was too tired to worry long. Next thing I knew, Lilliana was messing round in the kitchen making another big breakfast.

When we finished, Enrico asked me to take a walk with him. We went to the far end of the trailer park and stopped at a Scotty trailer, the kind that's rounded off like a big toaster. This one had sat there so long, ivy and tree branches were hugging it tight.

"V.J., I want you to meet someone. Nash Pickens. He's Hank's former brother-in-law, though Hank says he got along better with Pickens than his own sister. Nash isn't doing too well—his experience in Vietnam takes over a little more of his life every year. But something you said yesterday rang a bell with me. Something Hank had told me about Nash's early life."

From the look of his trailer, I was nervous about meeting this guy. But that fell away when a stooped, white-haired man came to the door. Enrico'd told me he was only about 50 year old, but he looked a lot older, like what we called worzels back home. Wizened people who'd spent too much time in the woods. "Nash, this is that boy I was telling you about. V.J., show him your drawings." Enrico didn't beat round the bush. I got the feeling we had only a few minutes with Mr. Pickens.

I stuck out my hand to shake, but he ignored it. I reached in my pocket and pulled out Nigel's drawings. When I'd unfolded them, Mr. Pickens flinched only slightly, but I saw something in his eyes. He knew them. "Do you know anything about these folks?" I asked.

He didn't answer, so I figured this was another dead end. Then I saw a big ole tear roll down his cheek as his dirty fingernail gently touched Mama Mae's picture. "Do you know Mama Mae?" I asked.

He nodded, which made a couple of tears splash on his dirty sweatshirt. I could just make out it said U. S. Army. "Do you know where she lives now?"

He still didn't say a word. I started to put away the pictures, but then he kinda growled. I guessed Enrico was used to him, because he translated for me. "Damascus," he whispered.

"Like in the Bible?" I asked, though just as those words popped outta my mouth, I remembered Luther had told me that was where Mama Mae grew up. I knew Luther'd lied about fixing the Merc, but I figured the stories about Mama Mae were mostly true.

Mr. Pickens shook his head and pointed to the ground. "Here! Now!"

"Damascus, Virginia," Enrico whispered, then said louder, "Thanks, Pickens. Come join us for dinner sometime." He squeezed Mr. Pickens' shoulder and turned us away.

When we were out of range, I told Enrico that someone else had told me Mama Mae was from Damascus. "Why do you think he added the words *here* and *now*?" I asked.

"Oh, son, it's hard to tell with Pickens. I wouldn't make too much of that."

"I reckon Mama Mae did something terrible to him," I said, ready to strangle that old bitch.

Enrico patted my back. "Probably no worse than any girl back then who broke a soldier's heart. He likely left for the war and figured she'd be waiting for him. The war did most of that damage you saw."

I told him that Luther'd said she'd been a wild thing. "Do you reckon he's Clayne's daddy?"

"Not likely. Didn't you say that Clayne was about twenty-three or twenty-four years old? Hank and I were working this out last night. The dates don't jibe. And when poor old Pickens came home, he didn't work, if you know what I mean." I didn't. Enrico looked embarrassed and added, "You know, down there. That's just part of his sorrows, but I'd imagine that makes memories of a girl break his heart even more."

"Well, she's still a bitch!" I said, furious that Mama Mae had wrecked another life, at least in part. As we headed to the Airstream, my comment hung in the air, neither one of us saying much.

When we got back, Enrico clapped my shoulder. "You're mighty young to be so cynical. Then again, I can tell you have a tender heart. You must be doing battle with yourself on a daily basis."

I wasn't sure how to take that, but it sounded about right. I planned to think on that some more—tomorrow when I'd be driving south. Toward home.

Della answered on the first ring. "Hey, you musta been right by the phone," I said, trying for lighthearted, even though I was nervous about my looming apology.

"Oh, I was just sitting here brushing Jake. He got into those damned cockleburs again, and he's been chewing at them and spitting them on the rug. Which I step on with bare feet! How's it going, Abit?"

"Not bad." Then I froze.

A little later, Della asked, "Abit, you still there?"

"I'm awful sorry about hanging up on you, Della."

"Well, I'm sorry about picking on your grammar. You've worked really hard in your classes, and now you can't even attend them. That must have felt like a stake in your heart."

Man, no wonder she was my best friend. We talked regular-like after that. I told her about meeting folks and getting fed. She thought that sounded like an improvement over my earlier reports. I decided not to tell her yet about giving up. It seemed that Alex hadn't mentioned it to her, either, or else she'd've been all over me like flies on stink. Just before I hung up, I added something I hadn't planned. "Oh, one more thing. About how my grammar stank?"

"I don't believe I put it that way."

"Whatever, I was thinking about it, and it seems to me I'm just doin' what you told Alex you were doin'— communicating." Back when she first moved to Laurel Falls, Alex kidded her for softening her crisp style of talking and picking up a few of our ways. When she told me about that, she said she'd told him she was "just communicating."

My comment made her laugh. "Honey, you got me there," she said. "You're right. Now just make sure when you get back to school you know the difference."

165

Liliana and Enrico invited me to stay another night. I figured I wasn't in a rush anymore, so I said yes, but only if they'd let me take them to a diner Hank recommended, as a way of saying thanks. It took some convincing, but they finally agreed, as long as they could leave the tip.

I wanted to make sure the café was good, and truth be known, I was missing the Merc. I hadn't taken it anywhere for a couple of days, and I felt the urge to be on the road again. Just after lunch, I headed down the highway to check out the place. It took about fifteen minutes of windy driving before I saw it up ahead, a neon sign blinking GOOD FOOD. That kinda worried me. I mean, if you have to *tell* people the food is good, how good could it be? And it was named The Windmill, but they hadn't bothered to put a small windmill out front or even paint one on the wall. The insides looked nice, though, with fresh upholstery and local artwork on the walls. Most important, it smelled good.

No one was at the register, so I picked up a menu to see what they offered. I felt my stomach rumble in a good way, especially when I read roasted chicken, broiled trout, fresh greens and other vegetables, and homemade rolls and pies. Just as I finished, a woman came over and sat behind the register. She had on a uniform with her name—Dolores—embroidered above one pocket. She wore a thick coat of makeup and her hair was in one of them beehives that went out of style back when I was a kid.

As I put the menu back, she smiled and said, "Don't see anything you like?"

"Er, I was just checking for later."

"Well, then, I'll see *you* later," she said and winked at me, flashing a gibbous moon of robin's egg blue eyeshadow.

I'd never been winked at before (at least not in *that* way), and I nearabout walked into the coat rack by the front door. As I hurried toward the Merc, I heard a truck pull up and someone shout, "Asshole!" I felt a stab of fear and turned toward a big, burly guy all red-faced in his truck. Then he looked over at me real sheepish-like.

"Er, sorry. Not you. Him!" he said, pointing at another truck that'd cut him off from a good parking place.

It wasn't till I got to the Merc and closed my door that it hit me. I'd gotten an apology from the type of guy who used to make my life miserable.

I was kinda dreading going back to the café, but by the time we arrived, the shifts musta changed, because Dolores was nowhere to be seen. We sat at a big round table, and oncet we'd ordered, we started talking like we hadn't just seen each other.

I was tired of jabbering about me and answering so many questions, so I asked them more about Canada. While we plowed through platters of food, they told me about Nova Scotia, where they spent spring and summer, now that they were retired from jobs dealing with tourists. It didn't surprise me to learn that Enrico had taken people out on fishing trips while Liliana had baked at several popular restaurants. I figured that was why that chocolate cake the other night was the best I'd ever had. It was runny like chocolate sauce on the inside and regular cake-like on the outside. I knew better than ask for the recipe. I recalled how Mama would throw a fit when someone asked for one of hers, though never to their faces. She'd tell them she'd get a copy to them sometime (but never did). Oncet they were out of earshot, man, she'd tear into them for asking. All I could figure was she had so little in life she took pride in, she needed to hang on to her recipes.

As we were leaving the café, I saw a poster on a bulletin board for the Old Timey Storytelling Festival in Duncan Mills—the same one I'd heard about on TV in Bennettsville. When Enrico saw me studying it, he told me that for his money, it was the best one in the state. That made the pull to go even stronger.

The next morning, I somehow convinced Liliana to let me do the washing up after breakfast. I did it real careful-like, because she used what seemed like her nicest dishes. She told me she didn't believe in packing them up in little padded coffins, never to be used. What was the point in that, she asked. I'd have to tell Mama about that one—her good dishes were like a shrine. Then again, maybe I wouldn't.

I felt sad as I packed the Merc and said goodbye to what felt like old friends. Liliana told me any fall or winter I was in the area to come back by. I believed she meant it. And I did, too, when I told them I'd try. Before I drove out, I thanked Hank for his hospitality. He wished me luck and gave me a couple of apples for the road. "One of those is for you, V.J. The other is for your teacher when you go back to school!"

Chapter 24

Enrico marked my map with the best route to Duncan Mills—a good day's drive southwest, but the festival didn't start for a couple of days, so I had plenty of time. Besides, I'd decided to stay on the road a while longer. I was enjoying freedom like I'd never known before, and I looked forward to seeing more of the countryside. I still had another week or so before Mama would worry about my whereabouts, and my money should hold out, if I were careful.

As I drove, I thought more about how folks were treating me like one of them, not the village idiot. I sent up a little prayer of thanks. Not long after, as fate would have it, I came up behind a car with a bumper sticker reading "Jesus Loves You: But I'm His Favorite." I chuckled for a good mile.

The closer I got to Duncan Mills, the more excited I got. I grew up listening to stories, and I'd heard festivals like that usually included some fiddlin' and good food. I was up for all three. The only real festival I'd been to was at The Hicks, where I met some of the traveling storytellers and musicians who liked to stop there between their bigger gigs. Gladys Robbins was one of the best, and I saw she was emceeing at Duncan Mills. She might even remember me, since I carried in all her bags and served her dinner a time or two.

The trip was taking longer than I figured, but that gave me time to think about what Enrico had said about me doing battle with myself every day. *Didn't everyone do that? Didn't Della or Mama or even Alex live thataway?* I wouldn't know any other way to be. Them hateful things people said about me (especially my first sixteen year) poured out like bats escaping their caves at night, repeating themselves over and over till my head ached. More and more, though, I'd started hearing the nicer things Della and Alex and some of my teachers said.

Even with the longer drive, I still managed to arrive well before the festival. Which was good, because I grabbed one of the last free camping places they'd set aside in a field not too far from the main stage. Since I planned to stay a couple of days, I set up the tent Alex loaned me (I had to laugh thinking about him camping!) and even tidied up the car a bit. As things turned out, I was glad I did.

Chapter 25

"Hello, Nigel? It's me, Abit, er, V.J. I hope I called at an okay time."

"Oh, hello, hello, world traveler. Yes, of course. How's the journey going?"

"Uh, fine. I guess. You remember giving me your card?"

"Of course, dear boy. Your call is always welcome, if that's what's worrying you."

I usually hated it when people called me boy, but coming from Nigel, it felt comforting. I couldn't reach Della or Alex, and I'd found his card when I cleaned the Merc. I'd gotten used to these calls of an evening; they settled my nerves. "Thanks," I said. "When I saw your card, I thought maybe you could help. I mean, your drawings have already helped a lot."

"Glad to hear that. What can I do for you now?"

"It's just the drawings are so good that I've gotten myself tailed by a pickup truck, beat up by a bunch of yahoos, and nearabout ambushed at a cabin in the woods."

I could hear him tutting and tsking as I told him more. Finally, after a long pause, he said, "As you know, I've spent some time in the, well, underworld here and back in England. I know firsthand the unsavory element you may have encountered."

"I doubt your characters were as bad as these. I'm not playing one downmanship, to quote Della, but I bet yours didn't spit tobacco, proudly carry shotguns in their trucks' back windows, and hate everyone who didn't look like them."

"No, mine just snorted cocaine, carried concealed weapons, and hated everyone in general."

I had to laugh. "You got me there," I said, then couldn't think of anything else to say. Truth was I *didn't* have anything else to say. I just wanted to hear a friendly voice.

"How's it going, V.J.? You sound troubled."

"I guess I'm kinda confused. It gets awful lonesome out here, just talking to strangers—or running from them."

"Why don't you tell me about some of the *good* people you've met?"

I filled him in on Jewel Johnston and Nadine, Enrico and Lilliana, Hank and Nash Pickens and started to feel better. I added how things were going okay until I ran into relatives and friends of Mama Mae and Clayne.

"I can well imagine," Nigel said. "Back in the day, those people who tried to catch me by asking around always failed. Word got out, and I could stay one step ahead of them. But the so-and-so who caught me went directly to where I lived. No warnings. Just direct action. She wasn't worried about proving I was guilty—she *knew* I was and figured she'd get the legal proof when she needed it. She found me after a few questions and a stakeout."

"How'd that play out for you?"

"That's when I was given the choice of imprisonment or working for the man. So my advice, V.J., is twofold. One, you've done your research. You don't need to ask any more questions—that will just stir up more trouble for yourself. You've talked to a lot of people—which was good, up to a point—but you've learned your grifters' modus operandi, their M.O. More specifically, you know a lot more about this Mama Mae character. Your mission isn't so much to talk to fellow victims as to *find* the perps. No point in poking the hornet's nest with a stick any longer. You'll just get stung. Cut that nest off at the base and then run like hell."

"I'm not exactly following you."

"Go find them, V.J. Forget Alex's list. You've got what you came for. And now, by way of your Mr. Pickens, you have a good idea about what to do next. But whatever you do, don't give up. You'd never forgive yourself."

I thought about what he said, and it seemed so damned obvious, I almost laughed. Why go on pissing everyone off, calling on more folks? And he was right about not forgiving myself. Something had been nagging at me as I was driving south; I *would* always feel disappointed in myself if I just went home. "So I should head over to Damascus, you reckon?"

"Yes, and though I cannot believe I'm saying this, talk with the cops. They're bound to know something about these grifters. Besides, you can't catch them on your own. You need their help."

I knew he was right, but I dreaded what that meant.

The next morning, I woke early to the sound of hammering and shouting and the general chaos of setting up a festival.

After all the asphalt I'd been staring at, I decided to spend the day walking in the woods not far from the campground. I loved feeling the carpet of pine needles underfoot as I looked for wildflowers and birds. The only thing missing was Jake. Walking in the woods (or anywhere, for that matter) without a dog just weren't right. I did spot several woodpeckers, chickadees, and other birds, including a migrating indigo bunting. At least that was what I thought it was. The way I saw it, when it came to bird identification, you went with your best guess—and stuck to it.

I found a nice mossy area for a nap and woke when one of the woodpeckers ratatat-tatted on a nearby tree. Back at the campground, I cleaned up in the park washroom and made a couple of sandwiches. I was getting low on supplies—and sick of sandwiches—so I looked forward to getting something at the festival the next day.

That night, I slept good in the tent and woke up feeling better than I had since staying at Alex's. I found a café for breakfast just down the road, and by the time I got back to the festival grounds, the crowds were pouring in. One look at that and, I had to admit, I wanted to turn the Merc round and drive away. I hated crowds. I didn't know what I'd expected—maybe more like the smaller versions we had at The Hicks. But I'd paid $12 for a pass, and I was beholding to Della and Alex for my money. I wanted to respect that. Without them, I'd be stuck in Laurel Falls with a ruined reputation following me like a bad smell.

I heard someone telling a tale from a nearby stage, and I headed over for a listen. I figured that would calm me down, but it was a story about a village idiot in a small mountain town. I felt disgusted by all the people laughing, especially since it wasn't the least bit funny.

I found another gathering where an Irish-sounding woman was holding court, not on stage but part of the more casual story-swapping that went on at these events. As I listened, I noticed a girl with red hair like mine looking at me funny. I looked away. When I stole another glance, she was watching the woman, swaying to the singsong of the storyteller. But the next time, our eyes locked, just for a second or two. I got this odd feeling and moved on.

As long as I was there, I decided to ask folks about Mama Mae and Clayne—not to find more of their victims but to see if the Ledbetters had been in the area lately. I figured my best chance would be with the ones who looked local, like the food and drink sellers. Holding up their pictures, I asked a pleasant-looking woman if she'd seen them. She told me to piss off. I showed them to a man selling barbecue, but he barked something about going to the lost and found if I needed to find someone. That smoky barbecue made me hungry, but I didn't want to buy from him. I found a shade tree where I hunkered down and, in relative peace, ate some odds and ends I'd brought along.

Until she walked past.

That red-headed girl was everywhere, though she didn't see me, this time. I held my breath till she passed.

As I finished my snack, I looked up and nearly choked. That bastard I'd talked to in the tavern in Bennettsville—one of the ones who beat me up—was walking toward me.

Damn! I couldn't believe they were so good at following me. My ribs started aching, just looking at him, and I felt as scared as I did that night. I watched him getting closer and scooched behind the tree. Then I ran over to the nearby stage area and saw a vacant seat next to someone wearing a flowerdy hat. I plunked myself down, grabbed her hat, and put it on my head. I turned to apologize and damned if it wasn't that red-headed girl. We were both so stunned we didn't say a word for the longest time. Then we burst out laughing.

By that time, I didn't see the guy anywhere round (maybe he was there for the festival, too), so I handed her hat back. It was a bright sunny day, and with hair and freckled faces like we both had, I knew she'd burn in no time. She put it back on and kinda stared at me, on and off.

When the storyteller finished his lame tale about possum hunting, I turned to her and said, "It's hard to explain, but someone was after me, and I needed a disguise. Thanks for the loan."

She just looked at me, and I could feel my cheeks burning. I guessed it was all the excitement from the guy and her, but I kinda barked at her, "Cain't you speak? Why do you keep staring at me?"

She swallowed, like she had to get something out of her mouth. "I don't know, you just look kinda interesting."

"Well, I hate to break it to you, but I'm not. Interesting."

"Who says?" I didn't have an answer to that. Then she added, "I'm Fiona. Fiona O'Donnell. What's your name?"

"Er, Abit," tumbled out without a thought.

"Rabbit?"

I laughed. "No, just Abit."

Thank heavens Gladys Robbins came over then. She smiled at me and asked, "Now why do you look so familiar?"

"Uh, we met at The Hicks, I mean the Hickson School in Boone. I helped you with your bags and such."

"Oh, what a small world! Of course I remember you. You play a mean bass fiddle, if I recall correctly." I was so flattered she'd remembered who I was I just stood there with what had to be a dumb smile on my face. Then she took Fiona's arm gentle-like and said, "Your aunt will be going on stage soon, and she asked me to come find you. She needs your help." As they walked off, Fiona called back at me, "Come to Stage Four at four. That's easy enough to remember. You can even wear my hat again, Rabbit."

I looked at my watch. Three fifteen. Seemed like forever till four.

Chapter 26

The word *smoldering* popped into my head as I thought about Fiona. I'd heard someone on TV refer to a woman like that, and at the time, I didn't know what it meant. But the minute I saw Fiona, I knew. Something about her dark red hair and big green eyes came together in a way that, well, smoked. I bet she didn't even realize the effect she had on others. It was just who she saw every morning in the mirror.

I worked my way through the crowd and grabbed a seat in the third row of Stage Four. The sun had gone behind the clouds, and what with the days getting shorter, the dark seemed to come down early. When the festival lights came up, the place felt even more magical. About four-fifteen, Gladys finally took the stage as the emcee, telling a tale about a revenant in the Smoky Mountains.

When she finished, she introduced someone named Chloe O'Donnell, the Irish woman I reckoned was Fiona's aunt and the same woman I'd seen earlier swapping stories. She came on stage real quiet-like, but she gave a performance the likes of which I'd never seen. We had good storytellers back home, but it took no more than five minutes to know that Ms. O'Donnell was in a different league. Her tale was a fanciful one about Celtic Druids, but what really caught my attention was *how* she told her story. She moved her body as though the story was deep inside her and to get it out, she had to move her hands, then a foot—

going off to the side like she was doing a jig—and then her whole body before moving just her hands again. She'd bob and weave as she talked and turned round, dancing to music only she could hear. In the middle of her tale, she took a musical intermission, stepping over to a hammered dulcimer and playing a folk ballad I'd never heard before. I later learned it was called "The Lover's Ghost."

It wasn't till people started clapping and the lights came up that I realized she'd finished. I'd been that spellbound. They started clearing the area, getting ready for the next act, and I had some trouble making my way out, I was so lost in her magic. And lucky for me I was slow to leave, because I ran right into Gladys and Fiona, who'd rescued Chloe from her fans.

"V.J.!" Gladys called out. "How'd you like my dear friend Chloe's story and ballad?"

I couldn't believe Gladys called me over to join their celebration. I was afraid to say much—I didn't want to fawn all over her and Ms. O'Donnell. Fiona had a wicked gleam in her eye when she sidled over and said, "I thought you said your name was Rabbit."

"Now that's an American name I hadn't heard before," her aunt said as she took my hand.

"Well, it's Abit," I said. "And that's just a nickname. My real name is V.J."

"Vijay sounds Indian."

"Oh, no ma'am. I don't have any Cherokee blood. Lots of people do back home, but not our family."

Gladys whispered, "She's talking about east Indians, from India."

"Oh, we don't have those either." They laughed at that, but it was the good kind.

"Well, don't you mind me," Chloe said. (She'd told me to call her by her given name.) "If you tried to pronounce some of our Irish names, you'd have a hard time of it, too."

"We're just going to have a bite to eat, V.J.," Gladys said. "Would you like to join us?"

It felt like ages since I ate, and the mention of food woke up my stomach. "Yes, ma'am, I would. What do you recommend?"

For some reason, they all three laughed again, though for the life of me I didn't know why. Chloe patted me on the back and kinda shepherded me toward the food tent, where they were serving all-you-could-eat soups and chili and heaps of rolls and cornbread. Gladys insisted on treating all of us, and I plowed through a bowl of each kind of soup and two kinds of chili. I stuck to the cornbread because I'd been missing that on the road.

Gladys and Chloe huddled together, talking about their performances and asking one another about how this sounded and how that could be improved. Which left me and Fiona to fend for ourselves. And, of course, I couldn't think of a thing to say. I had trouble round girls that looked like Fiona. Fortunately, she was a good talker, and I could've listened to her musical voice forever.

She explained that she was from County Connemara in Ireland, where her aunt was from until Gladys sponsored her in America. Chloe had settled in Virginia in a town called Galax and joined the storytelling circuit, something she'd done for years in Ireland. When Fiona added that she still lived in Connemara and would be returning in a week or so, my heart kinda cramped.

As she talked, I heard Della's voice prodding me to say a thing or two. So, I told her how I'd been taken out of school when I was younger, then went back to school at The Hicks, which was a special school, and then got kicked out. I left out the stuff about the con artists. What would she think of me—or America?

"Aye, Abit, I've heard a world of sorrows in your tale," Fiona said, "but one thing rings true."

"It's all true."

"I mean what stands out is that you go to a *special* school. I can see why." Man, that stung. I mean, I knew I'd used the word, but it was the way she threw it back in my face that hurt. I turned away, but she grabbed my arm. "What's up, laddie boy? I meant that as a compliment. You seem special, somehow."

"Well, here anyways, *special* can mean stupid, like that village idiot some jerk over there was making people laugh about."

"Jaysus, Mary, and Joseph! That's not at all what I meant. We're both speaking English, but it can be like a foreign language sometimes, can't it?"

Her face cracked open with a wide grin that made me start smiling, too. Then there was no stopping me as I told her about Della and Alex and Jake and the store. She shared more about Ireland, where she lived with her widower father. Oh, and she loved dogs, too. And her father ran a store in Clifden, so she knew a thing or two about the work I'd done.

I musta been lost in my thoughts about how much we had in common, because next thing I knew, Fiona was kinda shouting at me. "I'm sorry, I didn't catch that," I said.

"I asked you about the bass fiddle Gladys mentioned you played."

"Er, um, I guess I do. I'm really still learning it."

"Well, aren't we all? I love the fiddles and play all but the bass." She smiled again, like that meant something. "I also like to sing. Maybe we'll get a chance to perform with one of the pick-up bands here." I just nodded; I didn't want to break the spell and tell her that would never happen. At least not on my part.

We talked a while longer, but then I started yawning like a hyena. She started yawning, too, and patted me on the shoulder. "I'm gonna head on now and let you get some rest. Nice to have met you, Rabbit." She waved over her shoulder as she walked away.

That night I could barely sleep. I read more of *Ladder of Years* by flashlight, but then the batteries gave out. I had extras in the trunk, but I wasn't about to get out of my sleeping bag for that. I started thinking about Fiona, which was why I couldn't sleep, anyways. I'd probably bored her, but I'd had more fun than I'd had since … well, maybe ever. I couldn't think of another time this good. Way more even than when Clarice kissed me.

You'd think a campsite at a storytelling festival would be noisy, but oncet the din of people laughing and drinking had finally stopped, it was so quiet it kinda unnerved me. I got out of the tent to get some fresh air, and I was gobsmacked—Fiona'd taught me that word—by how many stars I could see. It felt like they were drawing me up toward them, assuring me that something bigger was going on in this crazy world.

When I woke, I pulled my sleeping bag to the tent's flap so I could watch the goings-on without getting into the cold morning air. Everyone seemed as happy to be there as I was. I flinched when I saw that guy again, the one who'd beaten me up, but he had his arm draped over some girl's shoulder. She didn't seem all that pleased he was tagging along. Whatever, he sure didn't look like he was trying to find me. If he was, he was one lousy detective.

Fiona and I met up at one of the food tents for breakfast, such as it was. Hard eggs, burned bacon, canned biscuits. But for oncet in my life, I wasn't thinking about the food. When I'd finished my coffee (which was actually a good brew) and Fiona gulped the last of her tea (which she said tasted like dirty socks, though I couldn't imagine she knew what *that* tasted like), we strolled round the grounds and talked. She told me she was scheduled to fly home after the next festival in Big Stone Gap, which was just down the road a ways. She was studying nursing and started school again soon.

I'd been wanting to tell her about my trip and why I was combing the hills of Virginia, and I finally got up the nerve. She looked troubled as my story unfolded, and I hoped she wasn't getting the wrong impression. As we walked, we passed one of them pick-up bands she'd mentioned the night before. I noticed a bass fiddle resting on its side. When they started playing "Footprints in the Snow," I stepped over to the bass and nodded at the fiddle player. Without missing a beat, he tipped his head, a motion that told me "Go right ahead." I jumped in at the second verse and played without a care whether I was any good or not. Ends up, I didn't screw up at all, and Fiona slapped me on the back in an approving way.

We wandered a while and eventually settled back at the now-empty tables round the food tent. A man was cleaning up the bins and wiping the tables. "You lookin' for someone?" he whispered.

"Here? No, I don't know anyone—well, except for Fiona and her aunt Chloe and Gladys Robbins."

"No, I mean out there," he said, jerking his head toward the horizon. "It sounded as though you was looking for someone."

I didn't know what to say. Nigel had me convinced I didn't need to stir up any more ill will by talking with more strangers. And I thought about Luther and the guys who beat me up and Clayne in his damn white pickup, so I didn't need another guy—this one about 100 pounds and three inches bigger than the last—coming after me and throwing me to the ground. "I might. Why're you asking?"

"Buddy, the barbecue guy? He said you was showing pictures around."

"Okay, but what's it to you?"

He stared at me with black marble eyes. "I maybe can help," he spat through tight lips, a little spittle catching on his bushy beard.

Oh, what the hell, I thought and whipped out Nigel's drawings. The man's lips curled back like a horse whinnying. "That's them all right. Sombitches took a lot of people with their scheme. A lot of us fell for it. Thing I can't figure out is why no one's caught them." He paused and looked at me funny. "What's in it for you? You a bounty hunter?"

Normally, I'd've laughed at something so ridiculous, but I decided I'd better stay on his good side, for a number of reasons. "No, they screwed me, too."

"How much they get offa you?"

I didn't want to get into all that, so I just said, "Plenty."

"Ha! Too embarrassed to tell me how much, eh? That's the way those crooks work. They prey on that; they know we don't want to be made fools of. By the way, my name's Stan, Stan Martin. What's yours?"

"V.J., V.J. Bradshaw."

"Sounds Indian."

I looked over at Fiona, who winked at me (twicet in one week!). I ignored Stan's comment. I had something else I wanted to talk about. Over the past few days, I'd been wondering why so many people in the middle of Virginia had been hurt by these folks. You'd've thought the odds of those three getting caught would've gone way up. I asked Stan.

"Well, they didn't do one then another, piecemeal. They caught a bunch of us in just one con and then got outta Dodge. And like me and my sister, most of the victims didn't file no complaint against them. I was in a bit of trouble with my ex at that time, so I didn't want to draw any scrutiny of my financial situation. Since then, in addition to sweeping up these storytellers' shit, I've got a good job at the wood-chip plant, and I'm catching up."

"So would you be willing to testify when I find them?"

He pondered that a while, rubbing his chin while he thought. His hand discovered the glob of spit, and he made a funny face, kinda disgusted. He looked at me as though I shoulda told him, but I didn't know him good enough, and I tried to convey that with my look back at him.

"Okay, yeah. Look me up when the time's right. Oh, and I think there's someone you really need to talk to."

I thought about Nigel again. "I've pretty much wound up my research," I said.

"Well, maybe. But this woman will definitely testify— and she'll kick some ass. She's just too busy to find them on her own, but she'll welcome your *research*." (He said that word kind of highfalutin, like he was making fun of me.)

He told me how to find her in Pikeville, Kentucky, but I doubted I'd go there. I said goodbye and hurried over to Fiona. I felt bad that she had to stand round and listen to all of that. And I worried that she'd think people here weren't willing to do what was right. But at least Stan had agreed to testify. For what that was worth.

Fiona and I spent a good part of that day together, and we joined Chloe and Gladys for a late dinner. Afterwards, I walked her to her aunt's trailer, and we chitchatted a bit longer. She gave a big ole yawn, and I realized how tired I was, too. When I stood up, getting ready to leave, an idea popped into my head, and I just blurted it out before I thought it through. "Say, where did you say you and your aunt are going next?"

"Big Stone Gap has a festival coming up next weekend."

"Hey, funny thing," I said, "I'm going thataway, too." I left it at that and headed to the campground.

By Sunday evening, the fairgrounds were a mess. It reminded me of a circus that came to Newland, a little ways north of Laurel Falls. (The same one where the mechanical fortune teller pushed a card my way saying I'd lose something important.) It was just a pint-sized circus, traveling from town to town, but still, it was a circus! We got there kinda late, and the show had already started, so unlike the way Daddy usually did, we stayed through till the end. Then he saw an old friend, and they were chewing the fat while the carnies tore down the tent and booths. I swear that was one of the saddest sights I'd ever seen. Junk all over the ground, a few poles still standing, an abandoned cheap toy someone won (or was gypped out of winning) lying in the dirt. Hard to believe it had hosted so much fun earlier on.

While I waited to tell Fiona goodbye, I walked round and kicked a can or two. I'd thought about picking 'em up, but that seemed like such a drop in the bucket, I'd leave it to Stan. When I was about to kick anothern, I heard a whimper. I looked round all the trash and abandoned tables, but I didn't see anything. I heard it again, and I walked past a tree and over to where the beer garden had been. I saw a little dog tied to a post, pulling hard at the thick rope round his neck.

"Hey, little feller. Whatcha doing tied up here?"

He looked up at me and squeaked for help. I bent over to pet him—he was just a little fiest, a scruffy, black-and-white eight-pound wonder—and he jumped up and licked my face like we were long-lost friends.

"Who's your friend?" Fiona asked, coming from behind the food tent.

"I don't likely know. Seems someone just left him." We both looked round, but only a dozen people milled about. Fiona said she was pretty sure the little dog didn't belong to them.

Something about that scene made me so sad—a mix of missing Jake and worrying about the fiest and, to be honest, saying so long to Fiona. "It sure has been fun to meet you," I said, trying to keep my voice even.

"Same here." She smoothed her skirt and then didn't seem to know what to do with her hands. She petted the dog, who, by this time, was wriggling like crazy in my arms.

"I know this is a stupid idea, but …"

"Yes, I think you should keep that wee dog. And it's a *her*, by the way." She smiled so sweet-like I would have taken a long walk off a short pier if she'd asked. I chuckled and looked down at the fiest.

"Okay, *she*'s a fine pup, but what I was going to say was maybe you could ride with me to your next gig in Big Stone Gap. I could use some good company, just for the day. Well, I mean, I could use some good company for more than that, but I'd only take a day of your time. I could camp here another night and start out when your aunt's ready to leave in the morning. I need to make one stop along the way, well, sort of along the way. But I could have you in Big Stone Gap by nightfall. And you could see more of America—I'm goin' to Kentucky!" It wasn't till that moment I'd decided to follow up on Stan's lead.

I was expecting her to laugh in my face, but she just ran off toward where her aunt was talking with some folks. At that moment, I felt so happy, I hugged the pup too hard. It let out a little grunt as its ribs pushed in like bellows. It was just a wisp of a dog compared to Jake, and I needed to be more careful.

"Howdy, Millie, how'd you like to ride along, too?" When I realized she wasn't a boy, I couldn't call her Duncan, like I'd first thought, but Millie worked just fine.

That pup started licking my face again, and then Fiona came back, laughing and kinda dancing round.

"You're on," she said.

And just like that I had a dog and a girlfriend.

Chapter 27

"The trees are my favorites," Fiona said from the front seat of the Merc, looking for all the world like a queen reviewing her empire. Not in a stuck-up way, just kinda regal as she sat there petting Millie, nestled in her lap. The mountains had finally gotten round to their full fall performance, dressed in orange and red and yellow with the pines adding some green. "Around Clifden, we have lovely beaches nearby but no trees like these. I especially love seeing them this time of year."

I'd decided to take the backroads so we could spend more time together, but I had to admit the scenery was a fine bonus. Fiona oohed and aahed as each bend in the road turned up a new vista. Until everything changed. Coal country. Even with the sun out, it felt dreary, like a constant sorrow hovered over it.

While still in Virginia, we came up on the Pittston Coal strike that had even made the news back home. We passed some miners on the picket line, and Fiona turned to study them. "Ah, these miners look even wearier than ours back home. The lines through their faces run so deep, they look carved with a knife." Then outta the blue, she blurted, "Stop!" Before I knew it, she'd jumped outta the car with Millie trailing behind her on her rope leash. I straightened out the car on the side of the road, parked, and walked back to the strikers' hut.

Fiona knew just what to say to the men. As she talked and asked questions, they listened careful-like. They invited us inside the hut, where a fire blazing in a big woodstove eased the morning chill. Except for the fire's glow, though, the hut was dark and smoky. As Fiona shared stories of the mines back in Ireland, the miners hung on her every word, taken by the way she talked. She told them how the mines in Ireland kept closing, leaving miners out of work and suffering from diseases like black lung. The men were all nodding, and a low grumble made its way round the hut. Mama's brother had worked the mines in West Virginia, and black lung was how he left this world, a decade ago.

When we got back in the car, Fiona made a growling sound, a combination of anger and frustration. "Those coal mining guv'nors are cold, cold round the heart." After that, we were both quiet for some time. Even Millie settled down and slept in Fiona's lap.

Twenty mile or so later, Fiona asked about my family. I told her Mama's maiden name had been McGovern, and her people were direct from Northern Ireland. Daddy's, of course, was Bradshaw, which was English.

"Well, good thing I won't be meeting them—what with the Troubles goin' on now. The British hate the Irish, unless they're Protestants in the north. Even then, they don't really like them—just want to keep them in the commonwealth."

I wasn't sure what all that meant, but she sounded hepped up about it. I'd've liked to learn more, but with only one day to spend together, I wanted to talk about other stuff. "We're in Kentucky now," I said. "It's a lot like back home only not as green, at least round here. And the towns aren't as good, in my opinion." And then I started laughing at myself. I'd never been to Kentucky, and there I was carrying on like some tour guide, as if I knew what I was talking about. I saw Fiona write something in the journal she carried everywhere, taking notes, I reckoned, to help her remember her trip. Millie woke up when Fiona was writing and kept trying to eat her pen. Then Fiona started giggling at the pup, and that made me laugh harder.

She hit me in the arm and said, "What? What are ye laughin' at?" I just waved her off. I couldn't tell her.

Later, though, we stopped laughing when we both started feeling the turns and twists on those mountain roads. Fiona had her head halfway out the rolled-down window. She might've been taking in the scenery, but I figured she was gulping for air, trying not to get car sick. The same way I was feeling.

We got to a straight section, and I pulled over at a wide spot. I needed to get out and walk it off. She followed and that little Millie did, too. (I sure hoped she'd be my dog oncet we dropped Fiona off.) There wasn't no view, so we just trotted round to let Millie run a little and got back in the car.

I musta been feeling real comfortable, because next thing I knew, I was telling Fiona all kinds of stuff. There was something about riding in a car together that made it easy to let down my guard. I recalled that happening with Della and Alex, too. "I don't know why it's so hard for me to make friends," I said. "I try to think about other people, not just myself. Be courteous-like. But then people say, 'Let's get together,' and I get excited and call and leave a message, but they don't even call back. Hard not to feel unlikeable."

"Oh, I know what you mean," she said. "The same thing happens to me." *Really?* I thought. *I can't imagine not calling you back.* "The world is a-changing; people think they don't need each other as much. Or that they can take without givin'. It's a sad state of affairs, if you ask me."

When I told her I'd always call her back, she hit my arm and said, "I would hope so, Rabbit." We both laughed at that, but I didn't think neither of us was joking. After that, we rode along talking about everything that popped into our heads. I asked Fiona a good bit about Ireland. I still had kinfolk over there, and I wondered if Larne was near where she lived.

"Naw, that's in Northern Ireland. I'm southwest of that. I don't venture up thataway, especially with the Troubles." She'd mentioned that before, so I asked her to explain. She told me about the two sides fighting against one another, her being Catholic and where my kinfolk lived being Protestants. At first, that didn't make any sense to me. Didn't they both believe in Jesus? But then I thought about the way people back home fight about being Church of God or Baptists, or whatever, and how one or the other was going to hell. That didn't make sense, either, but it helped me understand how people could hate and kill one another even when they believed in Jesus. Maybe especially. I ran my thoughts about Matthew 25 by her, and she nodded her head enthusiastically, so Catholics and Protestants could agree on something.

I didn't want to keep talking about that kind of thing, either, so I asked her to sing me a folk song. She thought for a while before singing one of the prettiest I'd ever heard. When she finished, she told me it was "The Fields of Athenry" about the Great Irish Hunger in the nineteenth century. That lonesome song and the way she sang it made us go quiet again.

We wound through the mountain roads a good while before Fiona broke the silence. "Kentucky looks pretty much like Virginia and Tennessee, though maybe a little more down at the heels, at least in these parts. Auntie and I just came from Tennessee, where it's lush with foliage and lovely vistas. She performed at Jonesboro—the biggest, baddest storytelling festival I've ever seen, here or back home."

"So the festival wasn't any good?" I asked

"What a pillock!" she said, laughing and punching my arm again. It was getting a little tender.

"What's that mean?" I asked.

"An eejit."

"What's that mean?"

"What you're being—a right idiot. Thick. Stupid."

My laugh caught in my throat for a moment, but then I sensed she'd meant no harm. Likely the first time I could laugh at being called an idiot, though you'd never catch me using that word.

It was early afternoon by the time we reached Pikeville. Along the way, we'd seen more strike signs, though Fiona reckoned these were miners in solidarity with workers to the south. But no question we were in the heart of coal country. According to Stan, the clinic we were headed to—Deep Creek Clinic—was the work of a woman who'd lost her father, brother, and husband to black lung. She started it on a picnic table at a county park with the help of a volunteer doctor who came twicet a week. Through donations and hard work, they'd moved into an old schoolhouse and added a food pantry and clothes closet.

"Who are we going to see?" Fiona asked as I parked the Merc.

"What you mean 'we,' white man?"

I couldn't resist using Alex's line on someone else, but her face made my laugh die real quick. "Sorry, just kidding. It's from an old cowboy-and-Indian TV show. What I mean is, I don't want you to get involved in this. One guy actually threw me out of his trailer—you know, his caravan." (She'd taught me that one earlier).

"How d'you know he won't respond better to a lass from the Old Country?"

"Well, first, it's a she—Esther Lally. And second ...", but I couldn't think of anything else. "Okay, but only if you promise that if things get rough, you'll run!"

"We'll see," she said and headed inside the clinic.

Chapter 28

Esther Lally seemed like a no-nonsense type of woman, which I reckoned was how she managed to turn a picnic table into a clinic. I couldn't keep from looking round at the modern offices and patient rooms she'd created outta nothin'.

"What are you asking me for?" she kinda barked at me.

"Well, were you swindled by three folks who looked like this?" I held up Nigel's picture.

"No."

Shit. Why did Stan send me here? I could feel my face get hot, a mix of embarrassment and anger. "Okay, wild goose chase. Sorry." I stood to leave, but Fiona kept her seat. I didn't know what she was up to.

I had my hand on the doorknob when Esther said, "It were just two." I realized then we musta passed some kinda test—thanks to Fiona. Mountain folks were that way, always testing to make sure you were genuine.

"What? Which ones?" I asked.

"The mother and boy. We were just getting established, about four year ago, and they came in all friendly-like and offered to help raise money. Back in those days, we had to stand next to the railroad tracks with a bucket—and as people slowed down, we asked for anything they could spare. I can't tell you how many rolls of pennies I took to the bank. But folks here knew we was doing good, so they gave what they could, including quarters and dollar bills, too." She stopped for a moment, as though she needed to gather strength to share what came next.

"Those two—they went by Clyde and Mamie Holliston; I'll never forget those names—offered to take over that task. They said they were new to the area and wanted to contribute. I fell for it. Oh sure, at first they faithfully brought the collections to me, and I was grateful I didn't have to stand at the tracks no more. I reckoned my safekeeping place was secret, but they musta watched me through the windows after I thought they'd left." She shook her head. "I'll never be that stupid again. We've got a safe now."

I didn't know what to say. Each story those two left in their wake was worse than the last. We sat there quiet-like for some time before she started up again. "I didn't want to report it to the police. I figured it would sully our reputation, and besides, the cops wouldn't do anything. Or, to be fair, *couldn't* do anything. They were long gone, and I didn't even know their real names. But I did mention it in a newspaper article about the ups and downs we'd had getting started." She pointed to the framed article on the wall. About fifteen other stories hung round it. Esther was a one-woman wonder, and the newspapers and magazines seemed to love telling her story. "So, I don't know how I can help you," she went on. "We got ripped off, I was too tired and embarrassed to go to the sheriff, end of story. Except for the fact that I still feel like a jackass for being conned."

"Any idea where they headed next, after they skipped out on you?" I was expecting the usual no-idea-can't-imagine answer, when she said, "Damn straight I know. And if I weren't so busy with this clinic, I'd've gone after them!"

"What? Where?"

"I asked around after they fleeced us, and a few folks knew their kin over in Wades Tavern in Virginie. They found out they'd headed to North Carolina to lay low. They'd ripped off too many people in Virginie and Kentucky and figured there was more money down there to fleece." She paused and thought for a moment. "Tell me, son. Just how many people have you been talking to?"

"I'd say about a dozen."

"And that's likely just a fraction of the folks they've hurt. Doesn't that strike you as odd? That they could rip off so many people and not get caught? And some of us now know them by sight and others are related to them, but no one has stopped them. What does that tell you?"

I shared what Stan had told me, about conning a bunch of folks and then fleeing. I also mentioned that folks were likely afraid of them.

"Well, yes, all that," she said, "but also that someone must be helping them. Someone with the law. Oh sure, I know firsthand how people don't go to the police after a con. But some do, and yet nothin', and I mean nothin' ever comes of it."

"I talked to one woman who said she went to the police and the newspaper, but they said Mama Mae and Clayne were long gone."

"But they keep coming back, especially to Virginie, where they was reared."

"I guess they move round—they ripped us off in North Carolina. And you're in Kentucky. So they don't stay put."

"Yeah, yeah, rolling stone gathers no moss, and all that." She sighed real big and put her hands on her desk to help her stand. I could tell she was in pain—both in mind and body. "I wished I could help more, but that's about all I know. Let me know if you find 'em. We likely won't get our money back—it's hard to prove how much they took— but I'd be willing to testify at their trial. I help a lot of our black lung patients take on those bastards they worked for in court, and we've won a lot of settlements. So I know my way around a courtroom. Count me in."

Thank you, Stan, I thought before saying, "Thank you, Ms. Lally. We'll do that. We'd better let you get back to work. And we need to get on the road. Fiona is expected back in Big Stone Gap before dark."

Fiona smiled at Esther, and Esther smiled back real big. That was the first and only time she'd smiled, which made her look about a decade younger. "You two keep me posted, ya hear? And good luck."

I wasn't sure if we'd ever get them caught, let alone in court, but I nodded. I rifled through my pocket for some bills to put in the jar she had on her desk. I thanked her again for her time, and we left. As it turned out, I'd come to wish I'd paid better attention to what she'd said.

We stopped early for supper before the ride down the mountain. I wanted to find a nice place, so Fiona'd think we knew a thing or two about good cooking. I found a decent-looking café with a deck, where, thanks to a warmer-than-usual evening for late October, we could eat outside. A hedge surrounded the deck, and towering purple coneflowers leaned over the railing. Some late-working honey bees were buzzing, dining on all the flowers, and I asked Fiona, "Why do you reckon bees buzz?"

She pulled a purple blossom close to her nose and asked right back, "How could they not?" Something grabbed my heart and squeezed.

We both liked what we saw on the menu and ordered a bunch of things to share: Brunswick stew, collards, pot likker and cornbread, fried okra (something Fiona'd never had before), and macaroni and cheese. It sounded like a real hodgepodge (Fiona called it a hotchpotch), but it all went down real good. We finished off with pie—Fiona got apple, I got pumpkin. Both were fresh. It was October.

I tanked up on coffee since I had a drive ahead of me. As I headed down KY 23 toward Big Stone Gap, the sun was fixin' to set, choosing pinks and oranges for this evening's show. Fiona was oohing and aahing again, and I agreed. Then we talked some and sat quiet some, and I took that to be a good sign. Of course, I didn't know why that mattered. I was taking her back, we'd say goodbye, and she'd travel to her home across an ocean.

We got to the campground in Big Stone Gap just before eight o'clock. Her aunt Chloe wasn't too mad at me for getting her back later than promised; she even invited me to sit round the campfire. We settled in and let its flames and heat lull us toward sleep.

Oncet everyone else had gone on to bed, we sat together a while longer. Millie, still being a puppy and all, got a second wind and started doing twirlies, running in circles and biting at her tail.

"That's how I feel right now," I said.

"I bet you do, because that's what you're doing. Goin' in circles." I looked at her funny and she added, "You need to do what you don't want to do."

"It's not like I'm *not* trying to find them." I was feeling uncomfortable, bordering on irritated.

She patted me on the back. "I know that. I think it's grand how you're out there talking with all kinds of strangers. But like your friend Nigel told you, you need to *find* those reprobates and get the law involved. Head over in the direction of Damascus. Something tells me that poor old man at the trailer park—the one who kept mumbling 'Damascus' as he stroked Mama Mae's photograph—knew on some kind of psychotic or psychic level where she is. And just maybe he was crying not so much because he missed her, but because he knew she needed to be stopped."

Chapter 29

"Where've you been? Alex told me about all those scofflaws after you, and I've been worried sick."

I knew Della wasn't so much mad at me as relieved when I called her on the campground payphone. I told her I'd tried but she wasn't home, though I knew I could've tried harder. I'd gotten sidetracked by Fiona and Millie. "I got me a puppy," I offered.

"Oh, and it chewed the cord on the payphone, I suppose?" I didn't say anything, and oncet her anger was spent, she added, "What does it look like?"

"She's kinda scruffy, black and white. And she just about never barks—just now and again says, 'yorp.' Sometimes I forget she's there, she's so quiet. That's unusual for a little dog, but I don't think there's anything wrong with her voice box. She's barked a time or two when the need arose. I can't imagine why anyone would leave that dog behind, but I'm glad he did." I went on about the storytelling festival but left out some details.

"It sounds as though you haven't done much lately to find those folks," she said, not so much in a scolding way, but still, she was calling my hand.

"Oh, I've been to Pikeville, in Kentucky, where I met an amazing woman who's agreed to testify."

"If you ever find them."

Now, that stung. "Hey, take it easy, Della. So I needed a break. I remember you taking some breaks—from the store and bathing and, and … oh, sobriety!" A few year ago, she really lost it a time or two when we had that crazy summer. Maybe it wasn't right to throw that back at her, but I'd been working hard except for a day or two. She didn't say anything, and I was worried she'd hung up. "Hello, hello. Della, are you there?"

Then I heard her chuckling. "Well, I see you've grown a backbone up there in Virginie." I knew she was joking round, pronouncing Virginia that way. "Okay, I'll back off," she added. "You're right. You did deserve a break."

I told her more about Stan Martin and how he pointed me toward Esther. We chatted a bit about this and that. Then she paused and something about the silence had me waiting for bad news. Sure enough, it came. "I got an angry visit from your mother yesterday. Andy, a little boy you were mentoring, called your house, crying. Wondering when you were coming back to school."

"Oh, shit! What did you tell her?"

"The truth. What you—and I—should have told her all along. She's a lot wiser than you give her credit for, Abit. Though she told me she should tan *my* hide for helping you hide this from her. I was the adult in all this, she said, as if your being twenty years old didn't include you in that category."

I was pretty sure that was the only time anyone had called me an adult. "What did Daddy have to say?"

"Well, Mildred and I aren't stupid. She didn't tell him, and I sure won't. I got her calmed down and told her how brave you are to venture out to find the truth. I explained that you were all torn up about being thrown out of school, and I think she understood. She got kind of choked up when she said she wished you'd felt as though you could've told her. But by the time we finished talking, I think she was on your side. You might want to give her a call tonight or tomorrow during the day. I see Vester going out most days after his midday dinner, so maybe you could catch her then."

It was late by the time we hung up. I wasn't about to call Mama then, though I knew the pending call would weigh on me. And I hated thinking about little Andy being so sad. That plus Fiona leaving, I doubted I'd get much sleep in the campground. I was surprised when a rooster woke me.

Over breakfast, Fiona's aunt treated me kinda funny. I think her mind started imagining stuff, worrying about what Fiona and me had gotten up to the day before. But by the time we'd finished our third cup of coffee with our bacon and eggs—cooked over the campfire—we were old buddies again. I told her she really knew how to make that campfire sing. She'd even made biscuits by burying a dutch oven in the coals, and I swear they were some of the finest I'd ever had.

The festival in Big Stone Gap didn't start for a few more days, but I needed to move on. It was late morning by the time I made myself say goodbye. I struggled to find the right words to tell Fiona how much I took to meeting her. She said she felt the same, though I figured she was just being polite. "And you know that first day I met you, Rabbit? All of three days ago, but it seems longer. In a good way." I nodded, and she went on. "Well, I wanted you to know I was staring and not saying anything because you knocked the talk out of me."

"I what?"

"I don't know meself. But when I saw you, I had one of those feelings I get, as though I've met someone important."

"Well, I hate to disappoint you, but I ain't important."

"Oh, laddie boy, you've got to work on that line. It's a bad habit, and I don't think you even believe it anymore." She hugged me and told me she'd let me know if she ever came back to America. I thought, y*eah, that and fifty cents will buy me a cup of coffee*. I couldn't imagine a fine girl like that remembering me, especially after she got home.

Chapter 30

"What's my best plan of attack when I get to Damascus?"

"Should I call on the cops for help if I ever find Clayne and Mama Mae?"

All the way down U.S. 58, I kept talking to Fiona, right out loud. I'd gotten a lot outta of our talks, and I missed her smart answers. And her. As I drove with Millie snuggled next to me, I swear I heard her respond. Maybe not right after I asked the question, but as I turned the wheel this way and that, her answers would come. When she told me I needed to call the cops, a shiver ran through me. For some reason, that started me thinking again about that damned fortune teller telling me I was fixin' to lose something important.

"Hey, there's a sign for the Carter Family Fold. Should I stop?"

I was surprised when I got an overwhelming *yes* to that question. One minute she was telling me to stop going in circles, the next she'd agreed I should stop off for some music. At least that was what I believed, and like bird identification, I was sticking to it. Maybe her summer in the South had connected her to our old-time music, and she loved it as much as I loved her traditional tunes. They were close in some ways, and entertaining in their differences.

And no one was better at old-time country music than the Carters.

I tried reminding myself I wasn't on vacation, but I kept hearing a voice saying, *you don't know when you'll come this way again*. I made a bargain with myself—I'd camp in the car to save money for my ticket. Then the day after the concert, at sunrise, I'd head to Damascus.

I nearly froze my ass off sleeping in the Merc that night, but Millie helped. She slept close and her warmth round my legs felt good. The next morning, I found a café near the center and warmed up with coffee and breakfast. The café was decorated with pictures of the Carter family and other famous musicians, along with some of their old LPs. Back at The Hicks, we played a lot of songs the Carters made famous: "No Depression in Heaven," "Little Darling Pal of Mine," and "Keep on the Sunny Side of Life" were just a few favorites. Mama Maybelle, her brother-in-law A.P. Carter, and his wife, Sara (who was also Maybelle's cousin), were what later became known as the "first family of country music." Eventually, they disbanded, but Mama Maybelle did a good job of training her daughters—June, Anita, and Helen—and they joined her on tour. Mama Maybelle was my favorite, and she inspired me to learn the bass fiddle, so I could accompany her on the records I had.

Mama Maybelle's guitar playing and sweet harmonies were playing in my head as I walked toward the family compound. I was humming "Sunny Side," a good reminder any day of the week, but especially these days. When I got up to the box office, I couldn't believe my luck—

Maybelle's daughters, who'd gotten back together after disbanding years ago (not long after Mama Maybelle died) were playing that night. I likely got one of the last tickets because all I needed was one. My seat was way in the back, but I didn't care. I was in!

I had plenty of time to kill till seven o'clock, so I took Millie for a walk in a wooded area not far away. I'd bought a dog leash (and a good supply of kibble) in Pikeville, and she seemed used to being on a leash. While we walked, I decided to change plans: I'd get a head start over to Damascus by driving right after the show; I could always pull off in a park somewhere to catch a little sleep. I knew that show would get me all hepped up—plus I'd drunk a lot of Dr. Pepper and coffee. When Millie and I got back, I fed her in the Merc, filled her water bowl, and headed to the show.

I was early, but people were already pouring in. I guessed we were all excited, like being on hallowed ground. It was hard to explain, but that music was deep in my bones, and I was on top of the world. I still had plenty of time before the show, so I looked for a payphone. I wanted to call Della before the evening got away from me and found one just outside the hall. Damnedest thing happened when she said hello. One minute, I was so happy I was fixin' to hear the Carters; the next, I felt so damn sad I could barely keep up my side of the conversation. A strange feeling I couldn't quite place.

"What is it, Abit?" I never could fool Della. Seemed like an age before I got the words out. "I don't know, Della. I just feel spent. And kinda lonesome, I guess."

"I'm lonely, too."

"How come? I thought you had more people round than you ever wanted."

"That kind of people, yeah. But I'm missing you. That kind of lonely."

"But I've been at school more than I've been home for the past three year."

"Yeah, but I knew where you were. And that you were safe."

And there it was, laid out for me. I was scared. Scared shitless. I didn't know what might come at me next or from which direction. Calling Della had brought all that up. But I didn't want to hang up, so I said, "Tell me something nice from back home. How's the store? Any good gossip?"

"Okay, let's see. Blanche has a new sign in the laundromat. It's more like a proclamation than one of her commands. Something like 'Do not wash sinful underwear here.' Whatever that means. And Duane's doing better. It's only been a couple of weeks since they split, but it looks as though he's getting more sleep. Oh, and Wilkie Cartwright? He's getting married in the spring."

I nearly dropped the phone. For nearabout four year, I'd sat next to that guy on the bench outside the store, both when Daddy owned it and after Della bought it. He was the shyest person I'd ever met, barely said a word. When Della used to ask him if he wanted some coffee, he'd just grunt, which we eventually figured meant no after the coffee she'd brought him went cold where she set it on the bench next to him. I couldn't even imagine him a-courtin', let alone married. What in the world would they talk about? But I was happy for him. And I figured if Wilkie could find someone, there was hope for me.

"Well, honey, that's all the news from this metropolis I can come up with. Alex and Jake say hey, and we all miss you. Call me again tomorrow evening to let me know how you're doing."

Turned out, I called her a lot sooner than that.

Chapter 31

I headed inside the hall. The stage was set, instruments in place, and lighting just waiting for the stars. When they came out, the crowd went wild, me included. Hard not to when they played all my favorites plus "Wildwood Flower" and "Can the Circle be Unbroken?" and a couple new ones they'd written.

At intermission, I bought some coffee but nearabout spilled it when I spotted Mama Mae and Clarice standing not twenty feet away. Not sure where Clayne was—probably out somewhere ripping off people and beating them up. I hid behind a pillar and peeked out, relieved to see them looking in the other direction. At first, I wanted to leave, but I'd paid for the ticket, and as I saw it, this was a chance of a lifetime. Besides, I kept hearing Fiona telling me to quit going in circles. Well, that circle *was* about to be broken.

The lights dimmed a time or two, and we all filed back in. I waited until I was sure they were already seated and thanked the heavens for my backrow seat.

The Carters came back on, and none of us could take our eyes offa them. But when they launched into "Wabash Cannonball," Clarice turned and smiled at me. Then she did that thing I'd seen on TV—making her pointing finger and bird finger into a V and going from her eyes to mine. I felt them waspers start up inside me again. Something weren't right, but I couldn't tell what.

When she turned back toward the stage, I slipped out. I dashed through the parking lot, and as I headed toward the Merc, I ran right past the Ledbetters' white truck. (I recognized it in that sea of pickups from the dent in its back fender.) In a flash of foolheadedness, I decided to see if they had any kind of ID in the truck to help me find where they were living. I looked round, and when I didn't see anyone, I tried the driver's door. It wasn't locked, same as folks did back home.

I quickly rifled around in the truck, but I didn't see anything except the usual mess—gum wrappers, fast-food containers, and the like—until I opened the glovebox, where I found some stashed mail. The address on each envelope was 233 Fitzgerald Street, Wyland, Virginia. I tucked one piece in my jacket pocket—an electric bill—and ran to my car.

Millie was all over me with happiness, and I felt the same toward her. I gave her a quick walk, followed by a treat, and then cranked the car. And the heat. Poor little thing was shivering. As I drove, I was lost in thought about Clarice and her sign language. After I got over the initial shock, I was pretty sure she was secretly letting me know she was glad to see me.

I pulled over at a wide spot on the right to check my map. I found Wyland, which was only ten mile or so down the road. At first I thought I'd check it out by daylight, but then I figured no point waiting till morning. As long as Mama Mae and Clarice were at the concert, and Clayne likely off somewhere being hateful, I figured I'd swing by while I was in the clear.

On the way, I pondered what in the world I'd do when I got to their house. Before I could finish that thought, I felt a hard push from behind. Then anothern. With the third blow, the Merc went out of control.

I couldn't get my bearings, like what I imagined being caught in a tornado felt like. I heard Millie whimper, and then the world went black.

I came to with Millie licking my face. She was favoring her right front leg, holding up her left paw. I checked it out and nothing seemed broken. I looked out the windshield and saw the car was caught between a couple of trees. I felt a stab to my heart when I saw how them trees saved my life— and Millie's. And the Merc's. If we'd rolled down the ravine, I had no doubt it would've been totaled. Make that *we* would've been totaled.

I sat there a while longer, trying to console Millie, who was shaking bad. Between her panting, I heard the engine tick, tick, tick. I must not've been out long if it were still cooling off. My only way out was through the back window, which was a good three feet closer to the ground than where the front of the car was dangling. I tried to move slow, afraid I'd jiggle the car loose and send it tumbling. I rolled down the window in the back and squeezed out. My right knee hurt when I landed, but still, I knew I'd been lucky. I reached in and lifted Millie to the ground. She seemed okay, other than her gimpy leg. I found her leash, and we walked a little, neither of us on steady legs.

The road was dark, and at first I couldn't recall where I'd been headed. Eventually it came back to me that I wasn't far from the Carter Family Fold, so we walked that a-way. Anytime a car drove by, I hid behind some trees, tugging at Millie to join me. No telling if Clayne was circling round looking for me. Yeah, Clayne. No doubt in my mind he was responsible. He musta seen me at the show and followed. And he musta traveled with his lights out, because I didn't see any headlights before I went off the road.

After what felt like forever, given my aching back and knee and the fact that I was carrying Millie by then, I found the payphone outside the Carter compound. I dug round for my wallet, where I'd stashed that cop's card—the one whose mama, Era Head, had lost $4,000. I recalled what Nigel told me I needed to do and decided to take Deputy Jenkins up on his offer to help.

By some miracle, the change in my pocket hadn't spilled out on the floor of the car, and I emptied it into my hand. I fed in the coins the operator told me I needed, and I heard a man say hello.

"Hey, Deputy Jenkins, I'm sorry to be calling so late. It's Abit, I mean V.J. Bradshaw. Remember me?" He didn't. "We talked about your mama losing $4,000, and how I was looking for the guys who did that?" That clicked. "Well, I think one of them just ran me off the road. My car's dangling from some trees, and I'm banged up. You mentioned you had buddies round the state who could help?" That came out like I was beggin'. I was.

"Oh, yeah, son. I remember," he said. "Gosh, I hope you're okay." He paused, and I was afraid he couldn't think of anyone, like he'd just been bragging. But then he added, "Let me call the sheriff over in Atherton. I'm sure he can help you—and he can be there or send someone in no time. Hang in there. Glad you called—well, what I mean is glad I can help." I gave him directions to the car, best I could. I heard him hesitate, like he wanted to ask me more about how my search was going but thought better of it, given the circumstances.

Millie and I walked back to the car, which didn't feel so far away on the return trip. We hid behind some trees and waited. And waited. Tonight's show at the Family Fold was long over and not much traffic was passing by, but we stayed hidden, just the same. I kept hearing a hoot owl carrying on, and it kinda scared me. Like it was warning of bad times ahead. After a while, I saw a cop car heading my way and waved it down.

He lowered the passenger window and asked, "You Mr. Bradshaw?" Millie let out a growl that startled me. I guessed she was spooked by all the goings-on.

"I am. Thanks for coming."

"Hop in the back, why don't ya?"

I was so happy to see him, I didn't think it was strange I had to get in the back. Maybe that was because he saw I had Millie in my arms. She was still trembly, and I wanted to console her best I could. When I closed the door, I realized the car had one of them grates between the front and back seats. Something felt off. I pulled on the door handle, but it wouldn't budge. "Hey, what's going on here?" I asked.

"Son, I'm taking you in. I understand you'd been drinking a lot at the concert, and we take DUI real serious in these parts. People get tanked up at these concerts and cause all kinds of trouble. Lucky you didn't kill yourself—and someone else."

"Wait a minute. You've got this all wrong. I was run off the road. By someone I believe is Clayne Ledbetter—living over at Wyland. Driving a white pickup. That's who you should be taking in."

"Oh yeah, it's always someone else's fault. I've heard it a million times. Now shut up and sober up, or you're going to make it worse for yourself."

"Give me one of those breath tests. I can prove I ain't been drinkin'." Those TV shows I'd watched for years finally offered me something besides killing time.

He ignored me, and we drove along with only that cop-radio gibberish squawking in the cold night air. I musta still been in shock because I should've asked him who told him I'd been drinking. But I just sat there as we jostled over those windy roads until I was afraid I'd get sick. (And it didn't help that the car smelled weird, like someone wearing perfume had been in there recently.) Finally, we hit straight road. A short while later, he pulled up in front of the jail.

"Don't I get a phone call?" I asked.

"Yeah, yeah, hold your horses." He turned me over to his deputy, who pushed me into a cell. While I sat there, trying to console my little dog and aching all over, Esther Lally up in Pikeville came to mind. I could hear her saying, "Someone must be helping them. Someone with the law."

Chapter 32

"Show me the breathalyzer results, or I'll call someone who can get this straightened out in a jiffy."

"Oh, yeah? Who're gonna call? Senator Warner? Oh, wait. I know, President Bush."

A couple of people shouting at each other woke me up. I'd been so tired from all the walking and worrying, I musta fallen pretty deep asleep. Millie, too, because she didn't even lift her head when all the commotion started. I looked round, confused, especially since it still seemed like the middle of the night. I recognized the deputy's voice—he wasn't the officer who brought me in but the one who jailed me. Oncet I shook off some sleep, I knew the other voice, too. I'd finally gotten to make a phone call, and, of course, I'd called Della. She'd said not to worry, she'd figure something out. I never dreamed she'd drive all the way up here in the middle of the night.

"Like I said, ma'am, unless you're his attorney, I don't have to show you shit. Hey, wait a minute, you can't just grab that phone. Now stop that dialing, I mean it …"

"Judge Weston, this is Della Kincaid. I apologize for the hour, but I remember you're an early riser." There was a pause, and she added, "Thank you, sir. I don't know if you're aware of this or not, but there are some rogue cops down in Atherton who are overstepping the law and stepping all over the rights of a colleague of mine." She listened for quite a while; next thing she said was: "That's right" and went on to explain my situation. Then I heard, "He wants to speak to you."

The deputy was yessiring and uhhuhing like a school boy in the principal's office. I heard him say, "No, there was no breathalyzer test, but his car ... yes sir. ... Uh, no sir, Sheriff Dixon didn't mention probable cause."

Next I knew, Della was standing in front of my cell door with the deputy nervously jangling the keys as he tried to find the right one. I had to dig my fingernails into my palm to keep from laughing. She hugged me and patted Millie, who was jumping as high as her little legs could carry her. We brushed past the stunned deputy without saying another word and out into the free world.

"How'd you find me?" I asked Della.

"Well, Mister, you're not the only detective in the family." Family. I liked the sound of that.

Della checked us into some historic hotel in Atherton. She said she was too tired to drive home—and that I needed a shower. I took a long one, with lots of hot water easing my aching back, but there wasn't much I could do about my wrinkled, dirty clothes. I knocked on Della's door, and when she said to come in, I saw her rubbing Millie's belly. We weren't supposed to have Millie in our rooms, but I couldn't make her stay in that dark old garage. Good thing she was such a quiet dog.

"I like the dog," Della said when I sat down. "And the beard."

I rubbed my hand across it the way all men seem to. "Yeah, I like it, too. Nice not to shave."

"Yeah, that's been a struggle for what? A whole year now?" she asked, kinda laughing at me.

"It's been more like three," I reminded her.

She walked over to her phone on the bedside table and called Alex to get him working on rescuing the Merc from its treetop perch. I got on the phone for a while, giving him directions and details about what had happened. I felt some of my tensions easing as we talked. He had that take-charge way about him that felt reassuring, at least most of the time.

When we hung up, Della and I went over what I'd found out, and I brought her up to date. Even though I'd already told her about almost everyone I'd met during our check-in calls, it felt right to go over it all again so she could get the full picture. I shared more about every stop, from Jewel Johnston to Esther Lally in Pikeville. And I showed her the electric bill with Mama Mae's address on it.

Then I mentioned the cop, Deputy Jenkins up in Bennettsville and how he'd betrayed me. "I cain't believe he'd do that—he's as bad as them cons who ripped off his mama."

"We don't know that, honey. He might not realize how crooked the lawmen down here are." That consoled me a little, but I still wasn't sure.

Things started looking up when Della ordered room service—ham and eggs and toast that arrived under silver domes, along with a silver pot of coffee and silver sugar and creamer. I'd never had room service before, and I took to it like gravy to a biscuit. We spent the day in our rooms—Della didn't think it was safe for me to roam the streets, since who knew if Clayne had been following us or his crooked buddies were keeping him informed. Thinking of that bastard answered one question I'd had. That sweet smell in the sheriff's car had been Clayne's stinking aftershave, the one the girls liked so much. That meant he'd been *in* the cop car not long before me.

For lunch, Della ordered room service again—steak sandwich and fries—and I was starting to think life was good again. She even ordered me a beer. This time I drank the whole bottle.

I asked her more about Mama, and Della explained how Mama had invited Andy Tomlinson—the boy who'd called her—down for the weekend. According to Della, she made quite a fuss over him and seemed to have forgotten she was so angry with me. That felt both good and bad, in a strange way. Next, I asked how the strike at the store was going.

"Things were heating up, and your timing couldn't have been better."

"Like I'd had any say about that."

"Oh, you know what I meant. Anyway, truth is, Billie is better at dealing with that stuff than I am. I'm too impatient. She even has a plan in mind, so I left all that to her."

We talked more and then Della made me call Mama. I was glad I'd waited because, like Della'd said, she wasn't so mad at me anymore. But after asking when I was coming home, she talked on and on about little Andy until I nearabout hung up on her.

That evening, Della and I watched the local news on TV. No mention of my mishap, but then, it wasn't exactly breaking news. Over dinner—room service fried chicken and greens and cornbread—we made a plan for the next day and called it quits. I was beat—we'd been up since five in the morning—and I used the connecting door to head into my room. Millie acted like she wanted to stay with Della, which kinda hurt, but when I snapped my fingers, she trotted along with me.

The next morning after the room service waiter brought up something called eggs benedict along with a basket of different breads and another silver pot of coffee, we slipped down to the parking garage and Della drove us toward Wyland. We stopped in a wooded area just east of town to give Millie a walk—a place off the road so no one could see us. She seemed to be over her trauma, because she was prancing round and acting happy again with no sign of a limp. Back in the Jeep, we made a few wrong turns, but eventually got to the address on the electric bill.

The old house was like any other out in the country— dusty white farmhouse with weedy grass out front. The yard looked like it'd been mowed recently, but there weren't any cars in the drive and no sign of lights through the windows. But maybe they hadn't paid their electric bill.

Della drove past and turned round. She parked a good distance away from the house. "I'm going to go check. You stay here. They don't know me, so if they come to the door, I'll just tell them I'm lost."

I didn't like her going alone, but she insisted, and her plan made sense. My heart was working overtime as I watched her walk down that road with no other houses nearby and then up the driveway. She knocked and waited. And waited. When she stepped inside, I almost lost it. I waited what seemed like forever. I was just about to go after her when I saw her come through the front door and close it behind her.

"They're gone," she said as she hopped back into the Jeep. "They left recently, though. I could smell coffee, and the food in the fridge was fresh. But they've cleared out. And they left this." She held out a note scrawled on the back of an old envelope.

Hi VJ
Sorry you missed us. Hope we never see you again.
Love
Mama Mae, Clayne, Clarice

Man, that hateful note pissed me off. We sat in the Jeep a while, not saying anything. I sure didn't know where to go next, and Della had just gotten on the scene. Which reminded me what all this was costing her.

"I hate that you're spending your money on that hotel and this wild goose chase," I said.

"It's wild, all right, but not a goose chase. We're going to find those bastards. This is the right thing to do. It's what you earn money for."

Della drove back to the hotel and pulled into the garage. I snuck up the back way with Millie, while Della stopped off in the lobby to tell them we'd be staying another day or two. Oncet we were all three back in Della's room, she asked me more about some of the people I'd talked to. I felt a strong tug to give her more details about Nash Pickens, the Vietnam vet, and how he'd known Mama Mae since they was kids, before he went off to war and maybe before she was living a life of crime. I told her how he kept pointing to her picture saying "Damascus. Here! Now!" with tears trickling down his face.

We talked about a lot of maybes. Maybe Mama Mae'd actually had one kind bone in her body and visited Mr. Pickens when she and Clayne were in the area, ripping people off. Maybe he knew what he was talking about, and like Fiona'd said, he knew she needed to be stopped. I'd kind of written him off, but he might've had insights I couldn't even imagine.

"Where is Damascus?" Della asked. "I thought I knew every town in this state." I showed her the map. "Well, I don't know anywhere else to look for them. You up for another road trip?" I nodded, even though I would've loved to hang out in that hotel room and order more room service.

We had a pretty drive through the mountains, the wind whipping a kaleidoscope of leaves across our path while stands of Joe Pye weeds waved goodbye to summer. It took us about thirty minutes to get to Damascus. Then we spent the better part of an hour taking roads one at a time, craning our necks as we looked for a white pickup with a dent in it. I figured there'd be a ton of them, but so far we'd seen only five white ones—and their fenders were in the same shape as the day they left the factory.

While we drove round, Della brought me up to date with things back home. Alex was working on a big story about a savings and loan crisis and Wilkie's wedding was already off. I didn't bring up the brouhaha because I knew Della didn't know anything new. After a while, we ran out of things to say and went back to concentrating on finding that truck. And then, just like that, I saw Mama Mae walking along the road.

"Stop!" I shouted. "No, don't stop. Not yet, anyways." Just like that fellow I saw on the highway as we made our way up to D.C., Mama Mae was sure to take a good look inside the Jeep. I scooched down into the footwell.

"What's going on, Abit? Should I stop or not?"

"That's her! That's her," I whispered. "Mama Mae, the woman who wore them diapers. The mother of Clayne."

I couldn't believe how cool Della looked as she passed Mama Mae. I saw her nod and do that thing everybody does to say hello without waving—lifting her pointing finger off the steering wheel, using the least amount of energy to be cordial. When we got a good distance, I tried to speak, but

227

my throat'd gone dry. I swallowed hard before asking, "You don't think she saw me, do you?"

"I don't, honey. I think you got out of the way in the nick of time. You've got good eyes. She didn't seem suspicious, and she doesn't know this Jeep at all. Though who knows what a grifter thinks."

"Did you see her?"

"Yeah, and she nodded at me. Didn't seem like she made any connection. I mean, how could she? She's never laid eyes on me." She paused a moment and added, "That was some getup she had on."

"Oncet I recognized her, I didn't have time to study what she was wearing. I was just getting out of sight. But now that you mention it, she sure looked a lot thinner in that hippie skirt than her baggy pants and diapers. And not nearly so motherly."

Up ahead, Della found a wide driveway and turned the Jeep round. She'd drive a while, and then stop when we were on a longer straightaway where Mama Mae might spot us. (I stayed crouched down, but peeked out, now and again.) I don't know how she knew this stuff, probably from her reporter days.

We tailed Mama Mae for a good ten minutes before she turned right into a long driveway that wound through a grove of trees. Della found a wooded place to pull in, out of sight. Lucky for us there was a decent view through a gap in the trees, and we could see her as she made her way up the drive. Della killed the engine just as Mama Mae headed into an old brick house.

We sat there for a good while, comfortable that we were well-hidden. Millie was just looking out the back window, and again, I was grateful she just about never barked.

"Okay, we know where they're living. For now. They could pull out again soon, though based on your Mr. Pickens' comment, it's likely this is some kind of home base. But still, I'd rather not mess around. Time to catch these scoundrels!"

"I don't know how," I said. "They're awful smart."

"And we're not?" she asked, raising an eyebrow the way she did when she was mad. Not at me. At Mama Mae and Clayne. "But I'm starving, and I can't think straight. Let's drive into town and get something from that diner next to the creek while the Ledbetters are settled in for a while."

We wound our way into Atherton, and Della parked the Jeep round back of the diner, overlooking Potato Creek, according to a small green sign. It was a nice view, though I thought I'd better sit on the floor again so no one spotted me. They'd definitely spooked me; I never knew when one of them would pop up. I put on a baseball cap of Alex's, something I never wore because they made me look stupid. I'd spent my life trying *not* to look that a-way, but at the moment, anything that worked as a disguise was okay by me.

Della came back with a bag of burgers and fries. She sounded disappointed that was all they had. After we ate for a while, she started laughing at me eating down in the footwell, with Millie trying to grab bites from my burger. I tossed Millie a few morsels to get her out of my face. When we finished, Della said, "Let's go back to our rooms and call Alex. We need a plan."

Chapter 33

Late that afternoon, I took Millie for a walk close by the hotel. We'd tried to take a nap after lunch, but Della and I were too hepped up about what we were fixin' to do that evening. At that moment, though, Millie was foremost on my mind. Things had been crazy, and she deserved better. She seemed happy enough, in spite of everything, walking proud on her leash. My heart felt full, like I got with Jake, and that's when I knew we were a pack of two. I couldn't believe this little dog was mine. I started sorta running and skipping, and man, that wound up that little dog like a top. She rabbited all over the place, so much so I had trouble keeping up. Her legs couldn't've been six inches long, and Alex's tailor told me my inseam was thirty-four inches, and there I was, lagging behind. It felt good to act silly for a while.

Speaking of Alex, Della called him when we got back to the room. She held the phone so we could both listen, and he gave us good news and bad. The good was he'd gotten the Merc towed, and they were fixing everything in Bristol, just south of where we were staying. The bad was they found what he called transfer traces of white paint on the car's rear end. Alex said he needed to know if Clayne's truck got any black transfer traces on it from the Merc.

"If I see some, should I scrape 'em off and …"

"No, Abit! Don't mess with anything," he shouted in the phone. Then he added, real quick-like, "Sorry. Just didn't want to jeopardize any evidence. All you have to do is let me know if you see any. Someone had swept the area where you went off the road. Very odd. And that means we have no paint flecks from the scene, which makes it even more important that we find something to take to law enforcement. If you see any paint traces, I'll get a friend at the state police to come take a sample that a judge will respect."

I started feeling a little sick when I realized that meant I had to sneak back over to Damascus to take a look. Without the black paint on Clayne's truck, we didn't have anything more to pin on these folks than Jewel or Era or Esther did. Alex said his friend was doing him a favor, and he couldn't ask him to come over for nothing. Made sense—but that only added to my dread.

When we hung up, Della took one look at my face and told me she was gonna do it. We argued for a while, with me telling her it was my fight and I needed to see it through. We kept at it until she won out. "Don't worry about me, Abit. I've been in capers like this before—even worse." I couldn't imagine, and I wasn't sure I believed her.

Next time I saw Della, she was dressed all in black—black turtleneck, black jeans, black boots, and black jacket. When Millie and I came in to her room, her back was to me as she put on a black watch cap and tucked her hair up under it. When she turned round, I nearabout screamed. Her face was streaked black, and I almost didn't recognize her.

"What are you doin'?" I asked.

"What does it look like? Blackening my face so the moonlight doesn't make it shine like neon." She kept scraping something across her face to fill in the streaks.

"Where'd you learn this? While a reporter?"

She turned back round and started laughing. I was so scared, I didn't see how she could think this was the least bit funny. "No, honey, on TV. I figured it made sense, though. The moon is almost full tonight, and there could be lights on in the house. I don't want anything to reflect off my face."

While she finished up, I looked round her room. She'd neatly hung up the rest of her clothes and her suitcase was stored atop the wardrobe. That was when I noticed the open bottle of wine.

"You ain't drunk, are you? That's not why you're laughing, is it?"

"No and no. I had to get the cork out of that bottle so I could burn it with this candle and make soot." I'd wondered why she had a candle burning. I thought maybe she was praying. "And I was laughing at myself. I know what we're doing is risky, but I feel like I'm playing someone on TV. Don't worry. When we get to that house, I'll be sober." I musta looked worried because she added real fast: "As in serious, careful, exacting. But I'll tell you, I plan to drink plenty of that wine when we get back."

Chapter 34

I'd sprayed WD-40 on the Jeep's door hinges till they purred and switched off all the interior lights. Nothing left to do but head to Damascus.

Della'd figured how to approach their house so she didn't have to pass it before parking. Not only would her Jeep be more familiar this time round, but thataway the driveway was on our side of the house. She could get to Clayne's truck without crossing in front of their big plate-glass window.

My heart raced when Della cut the lights and pulled off the road into that piney grove near their house. The lights inside were all ablaze, so Della'd been right to color her face. I was dressed all in black, too, but since she was the one going up to the truck, I didn't bother putting soot on my face.

If you didn't know better, you'd imagine theirs was a happy home. And who knew, maybe they were happy. Messing with people's lives, play acting, winning all them spoils. But I didn't reckon someone happy would go kicking people in the ribs.

When I saw how a bank of clouds had moved in and covered the moon, I tried arguing one more time that it should be me.

"But they don't know me," Della argued.

"Mama Mae does."

"Okay, I'll just tell her I'm lost—and then I'll look closer at her and say, 'Hey, didn't I see you when I was just pulling into town?'" I looked at her like she was crazy. "What?"

"Oh, and then are you gonna tell her you're in a hurry since you have to get to the minstrel show you're starring in?"

She put her hand up to her face. "Oh, there is that." We'd've laughed if we both weren't so nervous. "Okay, but all the more reason for me to go. I went to all this trouble." I nodded, both happy I didn't have to do it and sad I felt that way.

We sat there for a few more minutes, the sound of two people breathing all I could hear. (We'd had the good sense to leave Millie at the hotel.) I was too scared to speak, which seemed really pathetic since Della was doing the dangerous part. I think she was going over her plan in her head. I jumped at the sudden sound of her voice when she asked, "Do they have a dog?"

"They didn't when they lived at the school. I think a dog would cramp their style."

"Well, here's hoping their style isn't cramped now—because mine could be, in short order."

She eased out of the Jeep, the door barely making a whisper, and moved toward the house. In no time, I couldn't see her. I heard dogs start up at other homesteads nearby, but nothing from their house. Dogs always bark in the country, so I wasn't worried about that.

I didn't see her again till I spotted her dark figure slipping along the driveway and easing toward the truck. Just then, a man I figured to be Clayne came out the front door. Thank heavens the Jeep windows were up and it was too far away for him to hear me cry out, "Please, please don't get in the truck. Please."

He had his hand on the pickup's door handle when Mama Mae came out on the stoop and musta called him, because he turned and went back in. I could tell it was Mama Mae only because her height and hair were so different from Clarice's. Della moved from where she'd crouched by the side of the truck, and I prayed she was fixin' to get the hell outta there.

Before long, he came storming back out again, slamming the house door and his truck door. I lost track of Della when he raced down the driveway, turned, and stomped on the accelerator. Gravel spun every which way before the tires got enough grip for the truck to speed off. I could just make out the color of the truck.

I sat back up when he was outta range, but I still couldn't see Della. I nearly pissed my pants when the driver's door opened, and she slipped in, breathing hard. "Shit," she said as she crept behind the steering wheel. "There weren't any black marks on Clayne's truck."

"That's 'cause that weren't Clayne's truck. Or Clayne."

"Well, who the hell was it?" she asked, not shouting 'cause she didn't have the wind to. Just riled. "I heard Big Mama arguing with him. They were in the living room, and she was saying stuff like, 'Dammit, don't you go telling me my business. I know what I'm a-doing.' And Clayne, or whoever he was, yelled, 'Get off my back! I don't need this shit. If it weren't for me, you'd still be ...' They must have moved to a different room, because I couldn't hear their words clearly. They were really going at it when he went outside, slamming the door. Then Big Mama came out, calling him 'honey' and all, and I was sure it was Clayne, though I've never laid eyes on the SOB. That's when he went back inside—only to start arguing with her again."

"I couldn't make out who he was," I said, "but that was a cream-colored pickup—diesel. I could tell as it pulled away. And I got a strong sense it wasn't Clayne."

That was when it hit us. We had to go back up to their house and try to find the white truck. Maybe it was parked in the back. If I were them, I'd hide it, too, given all the people ready to skin them alive.

"Now it's my turn," I said. "I need to go up there and see if the white truck is in the back." I didn't even mind. It was time. Della nodded. She pulled off her watch cap and handed it to me.

I made my way real careful-like, heading toward the house by edging along the trees the same way Della had. Then I shimmied along the house toward the back. I couldn't hear much from inside. I guessed that argument spent their anger. When I got behind the house, I saw the white truck, reflecting the light pouring outta the kitchen window. My trip weren't near as scary as Della's, but my legs still kinda buckled.

The mist had risen and made everything feel extra creepy. I held my breath and listened as something rustled in the woods. Pretty soon I watched an old skunk slither across the driveway. I recalled the one I saw the night before Luther screwed up the Merc and I got beat up. That gave me a chill, like it was a bad sign. The skunk sniffed for a while along the other side of the driveway, then disappeared into the black unknown when the backdoor opened.

I jumped back along the side of the house. I didn't think I'd made any noise, and I guessed I hadn't. No one came a-lookin'. Whoever it was just stood there, smoking on the back porch. *Please, please don't come out here,* I thought, breathing as shallow as I could, even though I felt like gulping air. A cigarette flew through the air and landed in a puddle, its red tip sizzling when it hit the water.

I heard the backdoor close and the lock turn. The kitchen light went off. I edged my way close enough to the front of the truck to make out what appeared to be stripes of black paint on the bottom edge of the front bumper. I guessed Clayne was so certain I'd either died or gotten scared and run home, he hadn't tried very hard to get them marks off. There was enough black paint to satisfy that state policeman, or at least I hoped there was.

I moved real slow toward the front of the house and duck-walked back to the Jeep. Oncet inside, I started shaking. Della turned the heater on high, but it didn't help. I wasn't cold.

When we got back to Della's room, she called Alex and told him what we saw. "You can call your buddy, but he needs to get here as fast as possible," she said, her voice showing signs of strain. "No telling what Clayne might do with that truck tomorrow morning."

And she was right. After that, things started happening fast.

Chapter 35

"We had enough to get a warrant," Alex told us Tuesday morning over room service flapjacks and country ham. He'd driven up in the middle of the night. Man, those two were more than twicet my age, but they had more energy, at least when it came to chasing a story.

After breakfast, Alex drove us into town to get some books and magazines; we were going stir crazy waiting for news. As we passed the sheriff's office, I shouted "Stop!" A cream-colored truck—not the government kind but probably a personal pickup—like I'd seen last night sat right out front. I knew most trucks looked pretty much alike, but I had a feeling this was the one I saw at Mama Mae's. And that meant the sheriff might be her "honey."

Turned out he was. Well, in a way. Sheriff Dixon was her cousin, someone she'd grown up with. By Thursday, he and the Ledbetters were under arrest. Della and I drove over to Mama Mae's house to show some late-arriving agents with the BCI—the Bureau of Criminal Investigation— where they lived. We watched as Clayne and Mama Mae were perp-walked to one of the two state cars in the driveway. When I saw them bringing out Clarice, in handcuffs, I jumped out of the Jeep.

"Abit, don't go over there," Della shouted as I ran, leaving the Jeep door open. I needed to talk with Clarice.

She looked over my way as they walked her toward a different state car. She got this ugly smirk on her face and said, "Hey, Sweet Boy, are *you* behind this? Clayne said you were being a pest, but I never dreamed you could cause any real trouble."

"Yeah, but I told them you weren't really part of it," I said, running alongside, trying to keep up with the guy who had her by the arm. "I told them they'd forced you into fooling me."

Her words hit like a fist. "Oh, I fooled you all right, if that's what you want to believe. But that's my husband and my mother-in-law, and we're a team. A damn good team!"

"But why did you *give* me money? I figured you were sorry for all the trouble they'd caused."

She laughed. "I was sorry all right—that we didn't get more out of all of you. We just messed with your savings account to keep everyone off kilter." Then she stopped suddenly, making the agent miss a step and nearly stumble. She grabbed me by the collar and gave me the biggest kiss ever. This time, it didn't taste the least bit sweet.

The agent jerked her forward; I didn't follow. She musta known from my face that she'd taken me by surprise, because she shouted at me, just before they pushed her head down and shoved her in the back of the car. "You'll get over it, Sweet Boy. They always do. And maybe I'll look you up when I get away." Then she winked at me before looking up at the agent and adding, "And I *will* get away!"

As the car drove off, she waved from the back window, as if this was just another lark. I thought about all the things she'd told me back at the school, the kisses she gave me like she'd meant them. My chest had this strange hollow feeling, like if they took an x-ray, nothin' would be in there.

Chapter 36

Alex left early the next morning, before breakfast. Della and I took our time packing our things. As we carried them down to the Jeep, I looked longingly at the room service trolley sitting outside our door. Since we no longer needed to hide out, Della had wanted to go out somewhere for breakfast, but I begged her for one more room service meal. She laughed and said okay, but she couldn't eat eggs again for a while. I told her anything was fine with me. I was disappointed when I heard her order oatmeal and fruit, but I discovered that oatmeal with cream and maple syrup served under a silver dome tasted a lot better than back home. That plus three kinds of breads and a big pot of coffee. Man, I was going to miss all that.

When we settled into the Jeep and Della cranked it, I figured we'd head south to get home. But Della made a left turn, like she was going back to Damascus.

"Where're we going? I don't want to see that damned place again, ever."

"Hold your horses, so to speak." She chuckled at a joke only she got. I got it a while later when, after we'd safely passed Damascus, she turned into Mount Rogers National Recreation Area.

We were lucky to find a parking place since it was a Friday. Oncet we'd all piled out of the Jeep, we started walking the trail that led to where the ponies roamed. It took a while, but after all that time stuck in the hotel and stakeout car, we were happy to be moving, especially Millie. The temperature started dropping as the skies cleared, and we were reminded why there's an official color called Carolina blue (even though we were still in Virginia). I zipped my jacket tight, unleashed Millie, and started running, part out of excitement, part to warm up.

When we crested a hill, I saw the ponies, grazing on grassy slopes against a backdrop of mountains rolling into the sky. Della caught up, and we stood there together, trying to take it all in. It was almost more than the mind could handle.

As the wind picked up, leaves of yellow, orange, and red danced all round, while grasses—brown and tired-looking after a long summer—beckoned us closer. In one way, they signaled an end; in anothern, they were making room for something new. Like the foal we watched smacking its mama's sack, reminding me of that newborn calf I loved back at the school.

Millie was on full alert as she watched the ponies. We could have gone closer—I really wanted to hear them whinny and call out to one another—but I chose to stay back for a wider view. Some ponies had white stockings, others brown legs that matched the rest of their coats. Some grazed close together, while others wandered off, running free. And yet they were all members of the pack, unique but part of a whole.

As I watched them wander across the meadows, following their natural instincts, something powerful came over me. "I'm glad we didn't come here on the way up," I said.

"Yeah, you were pretty pissed with me, weren't you?"

I had to laugh. "Yeah, I was. With your lead foot, anyways."

"And why are you glad we came later, rather than sooner?"

"I don't think I'd've appreciated them like I do now." Della noticed something was turning inside and didn't say a word. She knew how to let things come out in their own time.

The sun went behind a white, puffy cloud, only to reappear brighter than before. For some reason, that reminded me of that day just before this crazy trip started, me sitting outside of Nigel's bakery wishing I'd been born somewhere besides Laurel Falls. I figured it was only natural to have those thoughts, but I no longer believed that kind of change would've made much difference in my life. Like those ponies—who could've been born anywhere, wild or in a barn, and yet they'd still be what they were meant to be—I was just who I was. I turned and shouted in the wind, "Don't be lonely. You have the whole universe inside you."

"So now you're quoting Rumi to the ponies?" Della asked, smiling at me in that accepting way she had.

"Nah, they already know that. Just reminding myself." Then I turned east and waved to everything and nothing in particular. Della's eyebrow went up, asking without words what I was doin'. "I'm just saying goodbye to lots of things and people that need saying goodbye to. Things I'm glad to get shed of. And to someone I wish I didn't have to say goodbye to, but enjoyed knowing. And I'm saying hello to my new life. And my new religion."

"Tell me more," Della said. I sensed from her tone she was worried I might've become one of those born agains who made life hell for everyone round them.

"Don't worry. It's a really simple religion," I said, "Just two words: Be kind."

"Ah, Henry James would approve."

"Oh, yeah? I don't believe I've met him."

"Me neither. But he's been known to say there are three rules of life: be kind, be kind, be kind."

"That's it! He gets it."

"And it's in keeping with what you told me about Matthew 25."

"Hey, you're right. I hadn't quite put those two together, yet."

Della waited a minute before saying, "Abit, that may be a simple religion to define, but it won't be an easy one to live."

"Tell me about it," I said. "I've already messed up a time or two, and I just came by it a few days ago. Like that deputy sheriff. I was hating him for locking me up, thinking all kinds of awful things about him, but he was just doing his job. It was that Sheriff Dixon who was the asshole." Della raised an eyebrow again, and I added, "Hey, I said I wanted to be kind, not blind."

We chuckled at my silly rhyme, but then Della added, "You do know your new religion includes being kind to yourself, don't you?"

I nodded, like I already knew that, but really, I'd need to spend some time pondering that. Then we went quiet again, just standing there, taking it all in. Long after we made our way back to the car, the feelings those ponies stirred held on. I couldn't shake them, and I didn't want to.

Epilogue

Christmas 1989

"Abit, check on the potatoes and then wash up for dinner."

Mama was ordering me and Daddy round. I didn't mind, but I could see Daddy frowning behind her back. She had a lot on her plate, so to speak, since it was Christmas Day, and she'd invited Della and Alex and Andy for our big dinner. (Turns out Andy couldn't go home for Christmas—his folks were both sick; at least that's what they said.) After we opened our presents—for me, socks and a wallet (they didn't know Alex had already given me one) and for Andy, a tooled leather belt—Mama had us push all the living room furniture to the walls and put up a big plywood sheet on sawhorses. She'd bought some pretty fabric printed with green holly and red berries that covered the plywood; when she added candles and some real holly branches I'd gathered for her, it looked like something in a magazine.

I'd come home again, like Delia in *Ladder of Years*. But unlike her, I didn't want to go back to my life as it was before. Oh sure, I got it that she'd changed the way she saw things, and maybe the folks in her life had changed some, too. But I wanted more.

Them ponies had cast a spell on me. I kept seeing them in my mind's eye, the way they ran free, but with purpose. They knew just what they were put here to do, and they were doing it. And that got me thinking that I was here for some purpose, and I wanted to find out what that might be. I'd felt like a no-count my whole life, and I was ready to look past that. I'd had a glimpse of the kinda life I believed I'd been put here for, and while I didn't know exactly what that was yet, I had some ideas.

And people round me were changing. Ever since Andy started coming to visit, Mama seemed different. I watched her fuss over him and help him do things. All I could figure was he allowed her to love him in a way she couldn't with me. That rankled sometimes; other times, it made life easier.

When I got home, Mama and Daddy were mad at me about not sharing my troubles and keeping my travels a secret. But eventually, they could see that they'd've had a fit if they'd learned I'd been thrown outta school. And when they understood what I'd done—traipsing all over tarnation for the truth—they felt proud. Daddy told me at first he thought it was just another one of my screwups (he didn't put it quite that way), but then he patted my back and said, "You've shown me different." I nearabout fainted, but I managed to nod in an appreciative way.

"Merry Christmas," Della hollered through the front door she'd opened a crack. We were in the kitchen and hadn't heard her knock. She was carrying two pies, and Alex, coming in behind her, had a big pan of dressing. Jake was following like a bird dog. I nearly dropped my teeth when Nigel walked in holding two bottles of what I thought was

Champagne. I was about to tell him he'd better go back and leave those at Della's when I saw they were sparkling apple juice.

"I cleared it with your mother," Della whispered. "I'd invited Nigel for Christmas after I learned his daughter was going to her in-laws. So when your mother invited us ..."

I told her that was fine with me; the more the merrier. I gave Nigel a big hug and took him by the arm as I introduced him to my parents and Andy, who was helping Mama with the cranberry sauce. I could tell Mama was taken with Nigel's apricot-colored velvet waistcoat and his polite way of talking. Daddy looked at him like he was from Mars, but then even he couldn't resist Nigel's charm.

Jake and Millie said their Merry Christmases the way dogs do, and then they both collapsed in front of the wood heater. We all found our way to the table, and Daddy said grace. He said all the usual—thank you for this special day and bountiful food. He even added thanks for new friends. But I almost lost it when he gave thanks for me returning home safely—as a hero! Talk about Christmas miracles.

I wouldn't call myself a hero, but I was proud to have stopped them three from hurting others. The cops even found a big stash of cash in their house in Damascus, and after some legal dealings, it was looking good for Jewel Johnston and Era Head Jenkins and Ila Pittman to get their money back. Alex was trying to pull some strings to get Esther Lally up in Pikeville something for her clinic and a small trust fund for Nash Pickens. Even though he hadn't lost anything (except his heart to Mama Mae), without him we might never have found them, so we figured he deserved some kind of reward. The legal folks said the trust fund, if approved, would be seen to by his former brother-in-law, Hank, for when Mr. Pickens might need a new sweatshirt or repairs for his trailer.

Then we did something I'd asked Daddy to add. After he finished his grace, we all went round and shared our own thanks. I said a prayer for the coal miners, which silently included Fiona, since she'd introduced them to me and, well, just because. Della was grateful to Billie for resolving the brouhaha—though she called it the "women's issue." She added that she hoped the women's husbands would start listening to them more. Andy and Nigel both felt lucky to have Christmas with such a happy family. (Good thing I wasn't drinking anything or I might've spewed it all over Mama's pretty table, though I had to admit, our family did seem happy at that moment.) Alex echoed those feelings, and Mama wound everything up saying she was grateful her boys were home safe and sound. I swear there was an S on *boy*. I recalled my new religion and let it go.

We didn't talk much as we passed the food round, but oncet we'd started eating, the conversation went all over the place. While everyone was busy with stories, Jake nudged my hand, and I gave him some bits of roasted turkey. Millie was right behind him, and, of course, I found more for her.

Alex stood up and tapped his spoon on his water glass and proposed a toast. (He was being a real good sport about having to drink apple juice.) "Let's drink to The Hicks, where Abit will be reinstated with honors and Andy will return with his mentor to guide him."

"What kind of honors?" Daddy asked.

"To make amends, they're awarding him a new scholarship that includes not only tuition but also full room and board, funded in part by the school and an anonymous donor. He'll be the first of many to receive it over the years." I was pretty sure Alex was the anonymous donor, and as for the school's contribution, I imagined he'd worked director Henson over pretty good.

Then Daddy really threw us all. "I saw Sheriff Brower the other day. He asked if my boy might consider going to school to become a lawman." Daddy was smiling like an eejit. The miracles just kept coming. I picked up the bottle of apple juice and studied it. "Daddy, have you been nipping on something or spiked this stuff?"

"No, son. I promise."

"Well, I've had my fill of detective work. Between Lucy Sanchez and Mama Mae, I've soured on that walk of life."

"I'll drink to that," Nigel said. *Lordy*, I thought, *let's not get into* his *walk of life*.

"Me, too!" Della chimed in, raising her glass for another toast. "I'm ready to run my store and keep my nose out of other people's business." Everyone laughed.

Della'd made a couple of pies—one pumpkin and one mincemeat—and Mama made something called Christmas pudding for Nigel. I thought it tasted like it had some kind of liquor in it, but that would be going too far for Mama. Or would it? I barely recognized her anymore.

That next week, Della hired me to paint the inside of the store and do a few chores that spruced things up. I guessed she wanted a fresh start to the new year and to clear out the bad feelings from the brouhaha. We had some good talks, just like old times.

On a break one morning, drinking coffee near the woodstove, she told me that my going out into the world to find my way had had a big impact on her. I shook my head in disbelief, but she went on to explain that I'd made her face how much she'd done just the opposite—withdrawing from the world. In fact, that was why she came to our little town in the first place. And yet, her coming to Laurel Falls had stirred things up, especially for the women who shopped at her store.

"I owe them something," she said after a moment. "I don't have to give myself over to them, but I do need to honor what I started, even if unwittingly." I told her I liked the changes she'd brought. "Well, good," she said, "because change has a way of keeping on coming."

She got that right. I was supposed to return to school in January, but the bad feelings that started on my trip hadn't gone away. I didn't think I could face that director again. Or the other kids, who figured I'd done something terrible enough to get run out of school. They likely wouldn't hear about how I'd found the people who'd wreaked all that havoc, especially since old man Henson wasn't coming clean about his dealings with them.

Alex had been gone a good bit, working in D.C. on some stories and following up on what was happening with the Ledbetters. He called Della every night and updated her. It had taken a slew of friends, favors, and colleagues to get things somewhat settled. That was how I found out that the cop—Officer Jenkins, whose mother had been ripped off— was a good guy, after all. He didn't know Sheriff Dixon in Atherton was so corrupt. In fact, he planned to drive his mother to Roanoke for the trial. And bring Jewel. The Ledbetters were up for attempted murder (of me!) and stealing. It was only because Mama Mae and Clarice were like wild polecats inside the house that they got arrested. If they'd played it cool, only Clayne would've been caught for attempted murder. But oncet they were behind bars, the investigation went deeper. And their cousin was singing like a house wren to lighten his sentence for being in cahoots with the Ledbetters (and arresting innocent people like me). He fingered another couple of lawmen in Virginia who were also taking money to look the other way.

I was still fretful about people like Clayne and Mama Mae. And Clarice, now that I knew she was just stringing me along to get what they wanted. Somewhere they'd taken a bad turn, fallen so deep into a hole that they'd lost sight of anything but darkness. Well, good riddance, though I wondered for how long. I believed they would be convicted, but I also knew they'd get out, eventually, and I hoped Clarice *wouldn't* look me up.

On New Year's Eve Eve, I was cleaning the storeroom when Della hollered that she was going out front to the mailbox. I heard the bell on the front door clang when she came back in. I looked up, and she was standing there with a big grin on her face.

"What?"

"Oh, nothing. Just a letter from Ireland." She handed me an envelope addressed to Rabbit Bradshaw, The General Store, c/o Della, Laurel Falls, NC. "Didn't you give her your address?" she asked, that eyebrow raised again.

"Who?"

"Come on Abit, you think I didn't know you were sweet on Fiona? Every time you mentioned that festival, I could see little birds above your head singing and carrying hearts." When I glared at her, she added, "You know, like in the cartoons. And maybe you didn't realize it, but you dropped her name a time or two while you were reminiscing."

I ripped open the envelope and skimmed real fast to find out what was up.

I'm spending the summer in America next year, and I was wondering if I could come see you.

I felt all the strength pour out of me and had to sit down. I mean, what if I'd built Laurel Falls up too much, doing my tour-guide thing? Maybe she'd find everything shabby and boring—including me. Then I noticed that Della was reading over my shoulder. I jerked the letter away.

"Oh, that's wonderful, Abit. You can show her all around and give her a tour of your school."

"I'm not going back to that school."

Della's face fell like a rock. All the mirth was gone from her voice when she asked, "What are you talking about?"

"I hate old man Henson's guts."

"That's only one person out of how many?"

"Well, what about the banker? He and Henson caused me all that pain just to CYA."

"That's two."

"And I'm not too keen on the rest of 'em. Nobody helped me out or checked on how I was doing. Well, maybe except little Andy."

"What about your scholarship? And Fiona? You wouldn't have met her if you hadn't taken your trip. Sometimes life's like that—the strangest detours lead somewhere unimaginably wonderful."

"Okay, that's really nice and all, but after I got to thinking about it and the day started getting closer and closer to going back to school, I just felt kinda sick. You always said to go with those gut feelings." She was really frowning at me by the time I added, "And besides, how do my trip and Fiona figure into whether or not I go back to school?"

"Well, as Fiona would say, that school might teach you how not to be an eejit the rest of your life."

"I'm not an eejit, and I don't need that damn school to teach me that."

Della looked struck. I knew she'd just been trying to lighten things up, but it fell flat with me. After a moment, she said, "You're right, honey. I shouldn't have put it that way. I just want you to be everything I know you can be." She ruffled my hair and added, "Promise me you'll sleep on it. That school and your trip have done you a world of good. Look at you, all handsome. A strong man now. Go back to that school and show them who you really are."

I laughed a little, embarrassed by her compliments. And grateful that Della and I could end this conversation agreeing on something.

I'd sleep on it.

Read an excerpt from the next book in the series following the Book Club Discussion Guide.

Your free book is "Waiting for You"

Want to know more about Abit and Della? Get your free copy of the prequel novelette, *Waiting for You*:

I've pulled back the curtain on their lives before they met in Laurel Falls—between 1981 and 1984. You'll discover how Abit lost hope of ever having a meaningful life and why Della had to leave Washington, D.C.

**Get your free copy of *Waiting for You:*
https://www.lyndamcdanielbooks.com/free**

Dear Readers ...

I hope you've enjoyed Book 2 in my Appalachian Mountain Mysteries series. I sure enjoy writing them!

I've been a professional writer for several decades now, and it still thrills me when readers write to me. Sometimes they have questions about the stories and the characters. Other times they leave reviews and, well, make my day!

> "Reminds me of *To Kill a Mockingbird* ... finding your books is like finding a rare jewel."
> — J.M. Grayson

Before I started writing fiction 10 years ago, I wrote more than 1,200 articles for major magazines and newspapers and 15 nonfiction books, including several books on the craft of writing. I'm now working on my fifth Appalachian Mountain Mysteries novel.

Book Reviews ...

I'm touched whenever people post reviews on Amazon, Goodreads, book blogs, etc.

> "FIVE STARS! Lynda McDaniel has that wonderfully appealing way of weaving a story ..."
> — Deb, Amazon Hall of Fame Top 100 Reviewer

I'd really appreciate it if you'd take a minute or two to leave a review. (It's easy—just a sentence or two is enough.) Reader reviews are the lifeblood of any author's career. Often readers don't realize how much these reviews mean to the success of an author. In today's online world, reviews can make a huge difference—so thanks in advance for posting a few sentences.

And Free Book Club Talks …

I'd love to drop by your book club and answer your questions—whether about my books, what inspired them, or even how to write your own books. We can easily meet through **Zoom** or other online meeting software. To keep things lively, I've created an all-in-one Book Club Discussion Guides to download **free on my website.**

I get a kick out of hearing from readers, so don't be a stranger! You can contact me directly at LyndaMcDanielBooks@gmail.com or through my website www.LyndaMcDanielBooks.com.

Lynda McDaniel

P.S. I thought you might enjoy an excerpt from the next book in the series (following the book club questions).

The Roads to Damascus
Book Club Discussion Guide

1. How does the title relate to the book's theme?

2. What do you think Lynda McDaniel's purpose was in writing this book? What ideas was she expressing?

3. What was unique about the setting of the book? How did the setting impact the story? Would you want to read more books set there?

4. What did you already know about the Southern Appalachians? What did you learn? Did you have misperceptions?

5. Abit meets a lot of characters on his journey through the Virginia mountains. Did they seem believable to you? Did they remind you of anyone you know—even if they're from a different part of the country?

6. Abit Bradshaw feels afraid and uncertain—but he keeps moving forward. Have you ever taken a hero's journey—either physically or metaphorically? When have you risked security in order to achieve something important to you?

7. What are the major conflicts in the story? Have you ever been taken advantage of by con artists (large or small)? How did you feel? How did you deal with your feelings?

8. What other feelings did this book evoke for you?

9. At the end of Chapter 19, Abit Bradshaw is staying at a tourist home. He says:

> *"After a while, I rolled over to look on the night-stand at the books guests had left behind. I wondered if I could get through any of them; my reading skills still weren't the best. One them kinda jumped out at me— Ladder of Years by Anne Tyler. I started reading, and the story grabbed me when this woman, Delia, left behind a life she didn't want to live anymore. Riding down a highway, not knowing where she was going, just like me. I didn't know what every word meant, but I felt a strong kinship with her."*

Have you read *Ladder of Years*? If so, how would you compare their two road trips? How did they end differently?

10. What did you think when Abit Bradshaw saw the ponies at the end of the book? What did they represent in his life? Have you ever had an epiphany like that?

11. Were you surprised by any cultural difference you read about? Have you been to any of the places mentioned in the story?

12. In Chapter 16, Abit Bradshaw talks on the phone to Della Kincaid. She tells him of a strike of sorts going on in Coburn's General Store:

"They're not really mad," Della said. "I think they're, well as you'd say, give out. Like when their husbands come in and make them take things out of their baskets and put them back on the shelves. And lots of these men are retired, but the women aren't. They still have to do all the cleaning and cooking. In fact, even more now that their husbands are home for three meals a day."

I'd seen what she was talking about. I remembered how women would come in and smile just being in the store. It really was a sight: cozy and special-like ... So those women would be all happy-like, or as happy as they could get, until their husbands came in and right in front of Della and me (when I was inside stocking shelves) told them to put those nice things back. Like those women were 10 year old. Some of them weren't even poor, like the rest of us ... Man, it was so embarrassing for everyone. And sad. I could never understand why their husbands were being so hateful."

Have you ever been humiliated by someone lording over you? How did you feel at the time—and how did you deal with it?

13. Do the characters seem real and believable? Can you relate to their predicaments? Do they remind you of yourself or someone you know?

14. How does Abit change, grow or evolve throughout the course of the story? What events trigger these changes?

15. Are there any characters you'd like to deliver a message to? If so, who? What would you say?

**Excerpt from Book 3 in the
Appalachian Mountain Mysteries series:**

Welcome the Little Children

1994

Chapter 1: Della

"I don't know what to do with this."

I was working in the back of the store, and I could've sworn I heard someone calling me. But when I looked out front, no one was there.

It wasn't the first time I'd heard phantom customers. Probably wishful thinking, though over the past ten years, I had built up the trade at Coburn's General Store, a small grocery I'd bought in Laurel Falls, N.C. (Not even the locals knew who Coburn was, but the name came with the deed. And no one would've called it anything else, no matter what I renamed it.)

I'd gone back to cutting a large round of cheddar into wedges when I heard: "I *said*, I don't know what to do with this."

That time I walked to the cheese counter and looked around. "Down here," someone barked. "I want to know how to use *this*."

I glanced down at a little girl dressed in standard-issue jeans and T-shirt who couldn't have been more than seven years old. Her round, full face framed by blond curly hair frowned at me as she held up a bulging can of chickpeas. "Some old woman gave this to us from the Rolling Store."

"Oh, I see," was all I could think to say. I'd learned that catch-all expression from my neighbor Mildred Bradshaw, perfect for times when I found myself at a loss for words. And the sight of a remarkably composed little girl holding a can of beans that could've blown any minute had that effect on me.

I stepped around the counter and bent down. "May I?" I asked, taking away the bean bomb and setting it on the floor behind the counter where it couldn't do much harm. "The Rolling Store took its last run out of Laurel Falls in 1990, so you've had that can at least four years."

"I don't know about that," she said, crossing her arms in front of her chest. "It was in the back of the cupboard when I was scrabbling for something to make dinner with. And like I've been trying to tell you, I don't know what to do with it."

"You'd better not do anything with it. It's about to explode, well past its expiration date."

"What a rip-off. You give away something that's no good." She punctuated her feelings with a stomp of her little sneaker-clad foot.

"I stand by my merchandise," I said, motioning for her to follow me. "Why don't you pick out something to replace it?"

Her frown eased as she wandered the aisles, picking up different items and studying them. Eventually, she grabbed a can and said, "I'll swap for this." A tin of Petrossian Caviar, something I stocked for a rich customer who ordered it more to impress her guests than a love of the delicacy. (Normally, no one else would be buying caviar at $90 a can, but this new customer was shaping up to be anything but normal.) I must have made a face at the costly swap, because the little imp started chuckling. "I was just kidding with you. I figured it was the most expensive thing in the store, whatever it is. How 'bout this?" She held up a $4 can of salmon.

"Let's make it two of those." I reached for another can and set them both on the counter. "How many are you cooking for?

"Four, though Mama doesn't eat much. But Daddy and my brother, Dee, eat plenty. I have to serve myself first to make sure I get enough nourishment."

Why is this child shopping for her family and making and serving them dinner? I thought. *And why isn't she in school?* Then I remembered it was Saturday. But still, something about the scene unnerved me.

She interrupted my thoughts. "I'm fussing over dinner because Mama's sick," she said, her hands on her hips, standing her ground.

I was trying hard to keep a promise to mind my own business. At least most days. A few years ago when I helped my next-door neighbor and best friend, Abit Bradshaw, track down a trio of con artists, I told everyone afterwards that I planned to stay clear of other people's problems. They laughed, but I'd managed to confine my enduring reporter's nosiness (from a former life) to friends and family.

Until now.

Something about a little girl cooking for her father and brother irked me enough to ask more questions. She beat me to it.

"I know what you're thinking. Why doesn't my father do the cooking? He's just awful at it, and I don't think he's fakin' it. And my brother is only a little feller. Dee's just six years old."

I looked closer to make sure she wasn't really a miniature adult. She was bossy and self-assured in a way I never was at her age. But I liked her spunk. "So, what's your name?" I asked.

"Astrid." She put her hands on her hips in a defiant way.

"Oh, that's a nice name. You don't hear it much anymore."

"Yeah, there's a good reason for that. The kids at school make terrible fun of it."

When I asked what they said about it, her face crumbled, and I could tell she was struggling not to cry. "I'll tell you what," I added quickly. "Let's not sully this space with anything from the schoolyard, okay?" She looked puzzled. "What I mean is, it's a lovely name in my store. You can consider this a safe zone." She nodded and relaxed her stance. "Why don't we have a Coke or cookies or something?" I asked. "I'm starving."

"Do you have anything that's not sugary? I haven't had any lunch, and I get a little dizzy if I eat sweets when I'm this hungry."

"How old did you say you were?"

"I didn't. But I'm eight years old. What's it to you?"

Wow. That little bruiser didn't hold back. If I were still a reporter writing profiles as I did back in D.C., I'd have started taking notes. I wondered again about her size and age—and worried she may not be getting the "nourishment" she needed.

I grabbed some of the cheddar cheese I'd been cutting and a few rounds of dry-cured salami, then sliced whole wheat bread and an apple. I set them on the table in the back and added a couple of fizzy waters. I wasn't sure if a kid her age would like the sharp cheese and peppery meat, but she gobbled it all down, as if she figured she'd better stock up while she could. But I also got the impression she'd be a force to reckon with at her own dining table—she positioned her elbows in a way that told me she was well-practiced at protecting her food. I had to scramble to get some, though I didn't care about that.

We finished our snack with coffee. I fixed hers like I used to for Abit—mostly milk with a slug of coffee. She drank that right down. When I opened a tin of chocolate chip cookies I'd made the night before, her eyes opened wide; she took two of the biggest ones.

While she ate them, systematically nibbling around the edges, I tried to think who she reminded me of. I chuckled when it hit me—Nancy Drew. I'd read all those books when

I was a girl, and I still remembered how composed and worldly she seemed for someone her age. I asked Astrid if she'd read those books, too, but she wrinkled her nose.

"Actually," she said between bites, "I prefer the Hardy Boys." She wiped her mouth on a paper towel and asked, "Do you have any recipes for what to do with that salmon (pronounced *SAL-man*)? I don't believe I've ever had it before."

After I set her up in the back with a couple of easy cookbooks and paper and pen, she got busy copying. I had to explain what some words meant, but otherwise, she sailed along. As I cleared our plates and cups, I asked, "Say, Astrid, would you like this tin of cookies to take home?"

Her face lit up, but just as quickly a shadow fell over it. "I'd better not," was all she said before returning to her recipes.

She was working away when I left to check on my dog, Jake. He was getting older, and I liked to bring him down to the store in the afternoon, once the nosy health inspector was safely on his way back to Newland after spot checks around the county.

As we came in the back door, I called out, "Hey, Astrid, I'd like you to meet my dog." Jake was already sniffing around, eager to see who or what was new in the store. But she'd left. Just a slip of paper on the counter with the words: THANK YOU.

A sadness crept over me as I read her eight-year-old's scrawl. The same feeling I had when I first saw her. I laid the note back on the counter and told myself I was being silly. She was just fine.

Chapter 2: Abit

"Whoa! Stop! You almost backed into the bandsaw I'm running over here. Dangerously close to being like the butcher who backed into his meat grinder and got a little behind in his work."

That was Shiloh. I'd hired him because, well, I was a little behind in my work. And he made some of the prettiest dovetail joints I'd ever seen. We'd met at The Hicks, or the Hickson School of American Studies in Boone, N.C. After my jaunt through the Virginia mountains to find con artists who'd messed with me and the school, I went back there to learn more about woodworking and wood carving. Two year ago, I moved home to Laurel Falls and set up my woodshop in a corner of the family barn. Next door to Della Kincaid, right where I wanted to be.

Della had seen somethin' in me no one else ever had, and I didn't want to venture too far from that. And she'd brainstorm with me sometimes when I was designing new furniture. So would Alex, her ex-husband and now boyfriend, when he wasn't in D.C. or somewhere covering a news story.

Even though my woodshop stood in the shadow of my parents' house, I liked working there. I'd taken out the dividing wall between two stalls so I had a good-sized space for making large pieces of furniture. The walls were mostly logs and chinking, but I covered one in rough-cut pine that gave me space to organize tools and what-nots. I added a strong floor so I had a sturdy place to set all them power tools.

At first, when I started building furniture, I didn't know what to make. But then I recalled the things that stirred me the first time I saw them—like that sideboard at Ila Pittman's while I was traipsing through Virginia. Or the dining table at Alex's. And hoosiers had always been a favorite, ever since I watched as Mama cranked the sifter handle under the built-in flour bin and it snowed into her bowl. Hoosiers also have a pull-out countertop for more room to pat out biscuits and a large cabinet below for storage. All them nooks and crannies gave me places to add special touches. Mostly carvings on the legs or at the top, but sometimes I'd chisel out a place for ceramic or enameled inlays from local artists. As more tourists and second home people came to live nearby, my business was on the rise.

Shiloh, aka Bob Greene, had a religious conversion of sorts while at The Hicks. He hooked up with some of the Buddhists who came there every summer, but unlike their serious devotion, he seemed to cherry-pick whatever suited him. He changed his appearance by dressing only in loose clothing, mostly black hippie pants and black T-shirts, and growing a long wispy mustache that gave him the air of a magician. That impression grew stronger when, after a meditation break, he'd slip into the woodshop without me knowing it.

Shiloh seemed to have specially taken to the notion of the laughing Buddha; he liked nothin' better than telling jokes. His repertoire was growing, though he repeated his jokes a lot, or at least I heard them over and over when different folks came into the shop. Even so, some of them made me laugh every time. Some of them.

I needed a break, so I headed over to Della's. I dusted off my overalls (I used to worry they made me look like a real hillbilly, but they were the best thing for the kind of work I did), whistled for my dog, Millie, and walked down the mossy steps to the store. It was a blustery day for May; I figured a rain storm was on the way. When I opened the front door, a gust of wind snuck in behind me and blew some papers onto the floor. I picked them up and read the top one.

"Hey, Della. Who're you mad at?" I shouted toward the back, since I couldn't see her anywheres out front. Millie, a black-and-white fiest who took up with me in Virginia, and Della's dog, Jake, some kind of yellow hound, were already tussling—their way of saying howdy.

"I'm not mad at anyone," Della said, carrying a case of homemade jams to the front.

I'd swear in the ten year I'd known her, Della hadn't changed a lick, but somehow that day, she looked different. It took a minute before it dawned on me she'd cut her hair to an inch or so below her ears, like she wore it when I first met her. Her hair was still that pretty reddish gold, though there were more gray streaks. But that was it. Me? I'd grown to almost six feet three inches and filled out a lot. Of course, I'd started as a kid.

"So why did you have this note by your phone saying ASS TURD?"

"Where?" she asked, a frown crossing her face. "That's not exactly my style of swearing, you know; I'm a little more traditional. Let me see that." She took the paper from me and turned it over. "Oh, for heaven's sake."

"What?"

"A little girl named Astrid was in here earlier, and she didn't want to tell me what the bullies at school called her. She skipped out while I was upstairs and left me a THANK YOU on this side of the paper, but I hadn't realized she'd written something on the back. Those bullies must have skewed her name to ASS TURD."

Oh, man, I knew what Laurel Falls bullies were like. Probably the same everywhere. And a name like Astrid was just different enough to whet their appetites. A dozen year back, they were mean about my names. As if sharing Daddy's name of Vester (with Junior tacked on to make matters worse) weren't bad enough, the nickname of Abit made them downright giddy. A bit slow. A bit stupid. Or a bit retarded when they really wanted to pile on. But who could blame them when my own daddy called me that? Not long after I was born, he told everyone, "He's a bit slow" to make *him* feel better, letting folks know *he* knew his kid wasn't as smart as most. Turned out, I learned a lot at The Hicks, and while I wasn't much good at math and such, I'd found my groove, you might say, in wood. That was about the same time I started telling people my name was V.J. (a nickname Della came up with).

"Laurel Falls Elementary is missing a bet," I said after thinking about ASS TURD. "You know how schools are always doing bake sales for new books or uniforms? Well, our school should set up a panel of 10-year-olds to judge the names parents wanted to give their newborn babies." I started laughing, imagining all them kids in striped T-shirts sitting at a table, discussing the merits of any given name, all serious-like.

I could tell Della didn't get what I was saying, so I went on. "Take the name Astrid. Her parents could've come to the school, paid $5 and asked the panel what would happen to the name Astrid on the playground. Those kids wouldn't even have to think about it—ASS and TURD would've come to them in the blink of an eye. Or remember that guy—head of the Forest Service—Richard Everhardt? I mean, what were his parents thinking? No wonder he was so grumpy, given what he likely put up with on the playground. No question they called him Dick Neverhard. And poor Mr. Peterson, the science teacher. The kids all said …"

"Yeah, yeah, I get it," Della interrupted, but she was laughing. "I think you're onto something, Mister."

"So who is she? Surely not a customer?"

"Well, in a way she is. She came in by herself holding an old can of beans, long expired after Cleva gave it to her years ago from the Rolling Store."

I'd ridden shotgun on the Rollin' Store for Duane Dockery back in 1985, taking food and supplies into the backwoods for folks who couldn't make the trek into town, a long tradition that went back a good fifty year to when the Rollin' Store started as an open-bed truck. But that big ole bus got to be a drag on Della's business after a while, and by 1990, Duane parked it for the last time behind the store. Della used it for storage after that. Too good to take to the scrap yard, she said, especially with Duane's fine paintings of flowers and vines on the side of the bus, which still looked good after all these year.

"Okay, but why was she in here all alone?" I asked.

Della filled me in on what she knew about Astrid and her ailing mama—news she'd gotten when she called her best friend, Cleva Hall, after the little girl left. Cleva'd retired from being a teacher and principal in the county, but she still knew everything going on. "She said Astrid's mother and father moved here some fifteen years ago to homestead, but neither one of them knew much about the land or living in the country."

"Sounds like you," I added, taking a big sip of the coffee she'd poured me.

"Thanks for the vote of confidence, pal." She smacked my hand as I reached for one of her chocolate chip cookies, but I knew she was just kiddin' around. Besides, I hadn't meant to sound mean. Della'd struggled a lot when she first bought Daddy's store, but she'd made her way better than most—outsiders or locals.

"Anyway, Cleva said her mother wasn't well; she got the impression it was not so much physical as mental. She's sad all the time, won't eat, and spends much of her time in her bedroom. The father is smart enough, according to Cleva, but there aren't that many places to work around here; he takes what odd jobs he can find. Cleva didn't know how they made enough money to live on, though the father may have some kind of trust fund."

"Next time ASS TURD comes in, let me know. I'd like to meet her," I said. "Maybe tell her how I used to be bullied—and that it gets better."

Within a couple of days, Della called. Astrid was back for more cooking ideas. As I walked down to the store, Millie in tow, I thought about how hard Mama had worked making our meals; that was a lot to put on a little girl.

Della introduced us, and oncet we'd said our howdy-dos, we started in like a house a fire. She petted Millie while I gave her some ideas about outsmarting them bullies and getting on with her life, though given she was only 8 year old, I wasn't sure how much "getting on" she could manage. It felt good to share my woeful tales in the hopes of helping someone else, though at some point, I started worrying all this might be too much for a little girl to carry. But she was drinking in every word, looking up at me like Millie did when I'd tell her she was a good dog.

When I was leaving, I heard Astrid tell Della to be sure to let "that boy" know next time she stopped by and added,

"He has some valuable information to share." I looked back and saw Della smiling. You couldn't help but.

A week later, I checked with Della to see when Astrid might be coming over because I wanted to talk with her again. She had a funny look on her face when she asked, "Aren't you a little behind in your work?"

At first I couldn't imagine why she was talking to me that way. Then it hit. "Has Shiloh been over here telling you jokes?"

She kinda snorted. "Just left. Funny guy, that Shiloh. But he's sure fond of patchouli, isn't he?"

"Yeah, he loves the stuff. It took me a year to get the old cow smell out of the barn—now I've got that to deal with."

"Well, I believe I'd take eau de cow to this," she said, fanning the air with her hand. "Which reminds me—I haven't seen your work lately, and there's something I want to order. When's a good time to stop by?"

"Shiloh's off tomorrow, so anytime. I'll air out the place."

I went over to Coburn's a few more times when Astrid was there, just to see how things were going for her. I was trying to live up to that revelation I'd had while on my trip through Virginia: be kind. Something I figured came to me from Jesus, from the way he lived his life. It wasn't that easy to do, though it *was* easy round Astrid. And Jake and Millie liked her, too. She was as crazy about dogs as me and Della. It was a nice time in all our lives. I wished it could've stayed like that.

Chapter 3: Della

Astrid came by the store several more times. She'd wave and toss out a quick hi before walking the aisles or looking through cookbooks. When I'd ask what she'd cooked the night before, she'd stop to think for a moment before judiciously recapping every step in her meal-making. I figured she was doing a good job because if a cook was pleased with her creations, her family or guests often enjoyed them even more.

Early on, we established that she could help herself to any drink or snack in the store (or "refreshments" as she called them). I wanted her to feel welcome. She wouldn't take anything when she first got there—she'd dig right in and get to work. In a while, though, she'd wipe her brow after so much exhausting work, like only a kid can pull off, and take a much-needed pull from a can of soda.

I got a kick out of her precociousness, and yet I'd've been happier watching her play softball or jump rope or whatever kids did for fun. But I consoled myself that she seemed to be enjoying herself, and I liked having her around.

One afternoon I needed to go to the SuperMart out on the highway. I didn't like to patronize that place—the father of our former sheriff owned it, and he'd always disliked me because I'd beaten him on the bid for Coburn's. (I guessed he'd had his heart set on a grocery monopoly in the metropolis of Laurel Falls.) Anyway, I asked Astrid if she'd like to go along so I could show her different cuts of meat (something I didn't carry), especially the cheaper ones that needed to be braised or slow cooked to make them tender. We had fun together—Astrid checked out every aisle, marveling at institutional-sized cans of tomatoes and all the glass jars of penny candy that rivaled anything from my youth. When I bought her an ice cream cone, you'd have thought I'd knitted her a sweater.

When we got back to Coburn's, Astrid took off on her old bike, which I could just make out had once been pink and festooned with colorful tassels (faded and brittle now). She'd told me she knew it looked "bedraggled," but it got her where she wanted to go. Which that day, I presumed, was home. She'd never mentioned where she lived, but I didn't think it could be too far from the store. I doubted she was strong enough to ride a long way over steep dirt roads. A few days later, following one of our afternoon sessions (school had let out for summer), a thunderstorm rolled through just as Astrid was ready to cycle home. I offered to give her a ride. She seemed nervous about accepting, but the rain looked steady and flashes of lightening concerned me. We loaded her small bike into the back of the Jeep, and I said, "Where to?"

"Not far. Do you know where Hanging Dog is?"

I nodded and turned right out of the parking lot. We rode along in comfortable silence until I asked, "What did you say your father and mother's names were?"

"I didn't." She crossed her arms over her chest.

I'd've chuckled if she hadn't looked so serious. "Okay, what are your father and mother's names?"

"Daddy and Mama." When I laughed, she did, too. A beat later, she said, "Enoch and Lilah. Enoch and Lilah Holt."

"Those are good names around these parts."

She stayed quiet after that. When I turned onto her road, she said in a low voice, "I'm not supposed to bring anyone home."

"Why not?" I asked, lapsing into my nosy self.

"It's tawdry." I loved that kid's vocabulary, particularly when she misused bigger words in a way that had its own logic. "But maybe Daddy won't be home."

No such luck.

Enoch Holt stood on the front porch as we made our way up their rutted driveway. As he loomed over us, Astrid became agitated. "I usually walk my bike from here. You can let me out now." I was determined to meet her parents, so I ignored her. "Really. Just let me out now," she said, her little foot stomping the footwell.

I parked close to the house and told her to run on to the porch; I'd bring her bike. It was pouring rain now, and I had on a raincoat. But she headed to the back of the Jeep and took her bike as soon as I got it close to the ground. She was already drenched as she pushed it under the overhang and hit the kickstand with her foot.

"Get inside and change, Astrid," her father said as she stepped up on the porch. He put his hand on her back and practically pushed her toward the front door. She turned and looked at me over her shoulder, then disappeared behind a closed door.

"Who are you?" her father asked. He gave the impression of being scrawny, not so much by stature as posture and attitude. His light brown hair curled down around the collar of a wrinkled linen shirt hanging over loose black pants. "Oh, wait," he added, "you must be that person who took my daughter to the SuperMart without ever asking me or her mother if that was okay."

For once, I was speechless. I could well imagine that any number of people could have told Enoch they'd seen Astrid with that woman from Coburn's—maybe when he was out on one of his odd jobs. And I got it that parents had the right to know who was driving their kid around, but they also had an obligation to feed her well and care for her. As I saw it, we weren't even close in the wrongdoing department.

"I'm sorry," I said. "You're right. I should have checked first to see if I could take her to that store. She came to me looking for cooking ideas, and I just thought of it as a fun trip to see different ingredients for dinner. But I'm glad you brought that up. Maybe you can explain why a little girl is saddled with so much responsibility for her family's meals."

He pulled on his beard. "I don't see how that's any of your concern," he said before turning and going inside. I heard the lock click into place.

The rain had let up, so I stood there a moment, hoping the door would fly open and Astrid would run out to play. I was surprised by how nice the house looked—a good-sized, hand-built cabin from one of those kits popular a decade or two ago. It had aged well, though it needed work around the deck and windows. When she didn't come out, I worried I'd gotten her in serious trouble with her father. Sure, I'd been reaching out to someone who'd come asking for help, but I knew I hadn't handled things well.

As I put the Jeep in reverse, I saw the curtain on one of the windows twitch. I looked closer as a hand opened the curtain wider and a woman's face pressed against the glass. We locked eyes and stared at each other for a few seconds. Then she let the curtain fall back into place.

That was the last time I laid eyes on Lilah Holt.

Welcome the Little Children and the
other books in the Appalachian Mountain Mysteries
series are available at book retailers.

Books by Lynda McDaniel

FICTION

Waiting for You (free prequel)
A Life for a Life
The Roads to Damascus
Welcome the Little Children
Murder Ballad Blues

NONFICTION

Words at Work
How Not to Sound Stupid When You Write
How to Write Stories that Sell
Write Your Book Now!
(with Virginia McCullough)
Highroad Guide to the N.C. Mountains
North Carolina's Mountains
Asheville: A View from the Top

24450725R00166